Love & Lies

August

For once, my alarm was a blessing. My mind had been on ultra-speed the last hour. Today, I start my junior year at a new high school. St. Andrew's Academy in Northern Illinois to be more specific. I hit the off button on my alarm and helped myself to a shower. After tripping over a box in my room, I found myself wishing I would've unpacked as my mother suggested yesterday. I found my suitcase and pulled out a simple outfit for my first day, jeans and a t-shirt. The cold wooden paneling under my feet turned to cold tile as I entered the bathroom and fiddled with the knob trying to turn the water on. Water began spraying from the shower head and soaked my hair before I could stand up straight and I sighed, stepping over the side of the tub into the shower.

The warm water relaxed me as I washed up and began planning out the day in my head. Before I could start running over my schedule the lights went out. I rinsed my body and turned off the water. I got dressed in the dark and wrapped my hair in the towel before I walked downstairs where I found the door under the staircase open.

"Dad?" I asked. He peeked out as I came around the stairs and bumped his head on the wall above the door frame. He was over six feet tall and that door wasn't necessarily accessible for people over five feet.

"Oh, morning," he said. His black, but graying, hair was tousled about as were his glasses which were down on the bridge of his nose allowing his brown eyes to see closer.

"Did you cut the power?"

"Ah… yeah. Accidentally," he responded. My dad was many

things, but handy wasn't one of them.

"Should I go get mom-?"

"Oh, no, no. I have it under control," he smiled. I cocked my head about to ask if he was sure but decided against it as I returned upstairs to run a brush through my hair, put on makeup, and grab my book bag. The lights came back on and I ran down the stairs.

"Aria, do you need a ride?" my dad asked as I went running past him.

"Um, sure," I responded. The school was only about a ten-minute walk from the house, which is why we decided on it. However, with them both being home while we get settled in, a drive to school would be nice.

My dad pulled up out front and I grew nervous. Teens walked around the grounds giggling, talking, and wearing nice similar outfits.

"Dad, they have on uniforms," I mumbled.

"Yeah. They should give you some information today. We'll get you the uniform and everything," he said. I nodded and took a deep breath.

"Okay."

"Have a good day," he said and kissed my cheek. I opened the car door and stepped out. As I was walking up the sidewalk to the old brick building, I could feel eyes on me. Not even two steps in the door and I was greeted.

"Miss Boyd, correct?" an older gentleman asked.

"Yes."

"Nice to meet you. I am Dean Rogers, welcome to St. Andrew's Academy. Do you have your schedule?" he asked.

"Yes, I do. I have first period in room 5B," I shared as I dug into my book bag. I already had the schedule memorized, but it looked like the Dean still wanted to see it. So, I pulled it out and handed the yellow sheet to him.

"Right this way. The main level is all A classes. B's are in the basement, and C's are on the second floor," he shared as we walked. "Your first teacher has our school policy handbook and just some other basic information to get you acquainted with us."

The Dean knocked on a door and a woman with her hair pinned up and bright blue eyes greeted us.

"Mrs. Milton, your new student has arrived," he said.

"Aria, welcome," she smiled and opened the door wider for me.

"If you need anything feel free to stop by my office," Dean Rogers added before making his way back upstairs.

"Come in, take a seat wherever you like," Mrs. Milton smiled as she wandered over to her desk. I surveyed the room and noticed there was only one empty seat in the back of the room. I made my way back and locked eyes with the guy who would be sitting in front of me.

"Nice shirt," he commented. I sat down and looked down at my shirt realizing my shirt contained my favorite group, The Ready Set.

"Thanks," I mumbled back. Mrs. Milton had several papers she handed me before starting class. I wasn't really focusing, though. Instead, I was looking around the room and noticed the uniforms were an ugly shade of pale pink and navy blue.

By lunch, I was comfortable with the building. Everything was easy to find. However, I hadn't talked to many people besides the guy in my first class and a guy who is my chemistry lab partner for the semester. I grabbed a tray of food and made my way to the nearest empty table. I ate in peace until three girls came over and sat down.

"You must be new," the one across from me commented.

"Yes, I am," I said, and the girls looked between one another.

"You're sitting at our table," another spoke. My eyes looked around the room realizing a lot of the other tables were full.

"Oh, I'm sorry," I began, not knowing how to react. They watched me as I collected my things and stood. I rolled my eyes as I turned around and bumped right into someone. I lost my footing and nearly fell as the person grabbed my elbow. My tray hit the floor and I looked up to see the guy from my first class. Milk from my tray had soaked my shirt and surprisingly there was nothing on him.

"I'm so sorry-," I said but cut myself short when I began to hear people laughing. I looked down to see my black bra was showing through my shirt. I felt my face get red as I wrapped my arms around my front.

"Noah!"

I looked behind me and saw the girl who sat across from me looking at the guy who stood in front of me. His eyes scanned over my face before he walked over and when he moved, more people began laughing as I ran out of the cafeteria.

By Monday morning I had my uniform and was ready to start my day. The walk wasn't bad and when I stepped into the building, no eyes were on me. I began to search for my locker and noticed it was supporting the girl from lunch's back as she made out with Noah. I sighed and tapped on Noah's broad shoulder. They broke apart and he turned to glance at me.

"Sorry, but could I get to my locker?" I asked. Noah straightened up, but this girl just stared at me.

"Jackie, c'mon," Noah said. The girl looked up at him and pulled herself away from the locker, shoulder checking me as they walked away. Not long after putting my things away, Noah appeared at the locker next to mine, spinning the dial. Wonderful, locker neighbors.

"Sorry about her," he said catching me off guard.

"It's not a big deal," I commented and shut my locker.

"My name is Noah," he said introducing himself.

"Aria, but you knew that," I said, and he snickered.

"Just being nice."

"Appreciate the gesture," I remarked and spun to walk down to the basement for my first class. Noah followed and glanced at me before he sat down.

Mrs. Milton was discussing Romanticism in the 19th Century when Noah stretched, and a folded piece of paper landed on my desk. The outer piece read,

"Aria."

I looked around and nobody was looking as I opened the paper and read, **"Which album was best? I'm Alive, I'm Dreaming or The Bad and The Better?"**

I pondered for a moment going over The Ready Set's music in my mind before writing.

"Feel Good Now is my favorite in all honesty."

I folded the paper back up and used the edge of the paper to tap his flannel-covered shoulder. He took the paper and it was a few minutes before he dropped a new note,

"That was a great EP."

I decided that was enough note passing and slid the paper into my notebook.

September

A week passed when the Dean had called me into his office. I walked in, my hands shaking afraid I had done something wrong.

"Miss Boyd, we review all our students' pre-examinations school-wide and we were very impressed with your writing portion," he began. I felt my body relax and smiled.

"Oh, really?"

"Yes, in fact, we wanted to ask if you'd be interested in tutoring or offering to help students write their papers?" he asked.

"Oh, yeah. Absolutely, I'd love to," I smiled.

"Wonderful. The librarian will contact you if anyone needs assistance and appointments can be scheduled through the library," he shared. I thanked him and returned to my classes as I took my usual seat behind Noah. I frantically attempted to catch up on the notes Mrs. Milton had plastered along the board already this morning. A few minutes later, Noah dropped a note on my desk,

"What kind of trouble were you getting into?"

I rolled my eyes and explained what had happened, receiving a note almost a minute later,

"Really? I could use help writing an entry paper for a few colleges…would you want to help me?"

I thought about my answer before writing,

"Contact the librarian."

I noticed his shoulders rise and fall, almost like a giggle once he read the note. This time he slipped me the paper as he stood. I watched as he wandered over to sharpen his pencil. I opened the note and read, **"You could just give me your #?"**

My face got warm as I looked over at him and he smirked. I shook my head and he pouted at me, mouthing a "please". I gave in and jotted down my number. He returned to his desk and snatched the note before he sat down.

I strolled into the lunch room and went through the line to grab food and decided to sit at a table close to the exit.

"Hey."

I looked up to see a tall guy with shaggy, blonde hair and green eyes.

"Hi, am I in your seat?" I asked getting ready to stand.

"It's a cafeteria, you're fine," he laughed lightly. "I'm Cadin," he introduced himself and sat beside me.

"Aria," I responded.

"Nice to make your acquaintance," he said and began to eat. "Where're you from?"

"Originally, Ohio."

"Really? I grew up in Kansas," he shared.

"My aunt lives in Wichita," I smiled as Cadin's eyes wandered behind me where Noah walked in folding up the sleeves of his red and black flannel. I peeked over my shoulder as Jackie walked up and took his hand.

"I gotta go talk to Noah," he said. I nodded and resumed eating while Cadin and Noah spoke. When Noah's eyes landed on me, he smirked.

"Could I sit here?" a girl asked me, pulling my attention away from the boys.

"Of course," I said.

"You're the new girl, right? My name is Christina," she

smiled.

"Aria," I replied.

"Ooohh, pretty name!"

"Thank you."

"Well, how've the first few days been?" she asked.

"Fine. Decent."

"I know you already had a run-in with Jackie," she said, and I nodded.

"She's kind of a bitch?" I asked, not really wanting to come out and state it.

"Oh, yes. Very. This place is a classic, horrible, cliché of any high school. Jackie, head cheerleader is dating Noah, the quarterback," she said, and I nodded with a slight roll of my eyes.

"I figured."

"Surprisingly, Noah's really smart. He has a 4.0."

"Really?"

"Yep."

My phone buzzed in my pocket and I pulled it out to read, "**My house, 6pm?**"

I looked up and noticed Noah looking at me over his phone.

"**I don't know where you live**," I replied.

"What do you plan on doing after high school? I mean, I know we're only juniors-," Christina continued our conversation.

"No, I get it. I'm interested in being a journalist, you?"

"Music. Have you considered joining the newspaper? I'm one of the editors. We could really use reporters," she said

"Oh, I'll look into it," I said, and she smiled. My phone buzzed again,

"**See you then**," below the message was a map link to his

house.

I got my homework done and my mom came home before my dad with several grocery bags in her hands. I helped her set them down on the counter and began unbagging them with her.

"Hey mom, could you give me a ride?" I asked.

"Where to?"

"Um, Rockford Boulevard? I'm tutoring someone tonight," I shared.

"Really? Who?" she asked. I cringed wishing she wouldn't have asked.

"His name is Noah."

"It's a *he*?"

"Yeah, but no need to worry. He has a girlfriend."

"That doesn't mean anything, Aria. You know that. Are his parents going to be home?"

"Mom, I don't know," I sighed. She watched me a moment before shaking her head and letting out a deep breath as well.

"Fine," she said.

When my mom pulled down the driveway, my eyes widened. The house was a beautiful one story, rustic looking home. As I went to climb out, Noah approached.

"Hello Mrs. Boyd," Noah said to my mom.

"He looks a lot older," my mom whispered to me before saying hello to Noah. I looked at my mom and could tell she was nervous for me.

"Bye Mom," I said and shut the door to her 2005 Trailblazer.

"Nice house," I said to Noah as he walked up the sidewalk with me.

"Thanks," he smiled and opened the door for me. "We can go right in here," he said and motioned to a dark themed living room. He had a MacBook on the coffee table, a water bottle, textbooks, and notebooks scattered about. The tie from his uniform was loosened and his sleeves were rolled up to his elbows. He was cute... Really cute. His brown hair was falling into his eyes and I looked away, not wanting to stare at him any longer.

"Looks like you've been busy," I commented.

"I got home about a half-hour ago. Practice was cut short today," he said and sat on the couch. I joined him, and he moved the blanket he had between us.

"You mentioned needing help with a paper?" I asked trying to stay on track.

"Yeah. It's already written. I just want to make sure it reads okay," he said and moved a few notebooks to find a folder. In it was several pamphlets for universities. "There are five papers though," he revealed.

"Let me see," I said, and he handed over the folder. As I read, he was doing math homework, occasionally the sound of his fingers tapping the keys on his calculator filled the house. After reading the first essay, I learned that Noah wanted to go into Photojournalism. He said a lot about how he was hard working, efficient, and a quick learner. He wanted to open his own media production company. I couldn't help but admit that I was impressed. He said he was a photographer and could edit footage very well.

"This is amazing," I began. His brown eyes found mine and he looked down at the paper.

"But?"

"You only have a few grammatical errors," I shared and went over the mistakes with him. Repeating the process for the other four papers was a lot more exhausting than I had originally expected.

"Thank you," he said as he put away his last paper.

"No problem," I shrugged and looked at the clock, 8:57pm. "I should probably call my mom-."

"No, let me drive you?" he offered.

"You sure?"

"Yeah," he said and stood up grabbing a black leather jacket and sliding it on. I followed him out the front door and ran into him when he stopped.

"Oh- sorry," I said to him quietly.

"Where are you going?" an older man asked before noticing me. It was clearly Noah's dad, they looked a lot alike. "Oh, hello," he said to me.

"Hi."

"I'm running her home," Noah said.

"Alright," his dad shrugged and slid past us to get inside. I'll admit I was expecting his dad to ask me to introduce myself. I snapped out of my thoughts when Noah held a helmet out to me.

"Um," I looked at the blue motorcycle and rose my eyebrows.

"What?" he asked.

"I'm not... Um..." I began.

"You'll be fine, just hold onto me," he said. I climbed on behind him and put my hands on my thighs, afraid to touch him. What if he could tell I was starting to find him attractive? He revved the engine before driving off which startled me. I quickly wrapped my arms around his torso and held the helmet tight to my head. I directed him to my house and we pulled up in my driveway... thankfully, in one piece.

"Thanks for the ride," I said as I climbed off and removed the helmet.

"Anytime. It wasn't so bad, was it?" he laughed lightly.

"I guess not," I laughed in return. Noah smiled and motioned up to the house.

"Should I talk to your parents?"

"No. I'm home, they'll be happy."

"Okay," he said. I went to walk up to the house, but before I could get too far, Noah spoke.

"Aria, um, Mrs. Milton gave us that assignment today. Maybe you could help me with it tomorrow after school?"

"Don't you have practice?"

"Academics first," he said. I pondered for a moment. "I'll drive you to my place and afterwards bring you home," he added.

"Sure," I replied.

"Awesome. Goodnight, Aria," he said.

"Night," I answered and walked up the sidewalk and into the house. My mom came out from the kitchen and looked at me.

"Are you okay?" she asked.

"Yeah. Perfect."

When I walked into the cafeteria the next day, I looked around for Noah, wanting to make sure he was still planning on meeting after school. I didn't know why, but I was excited. Well, I knew why. Noah came in and I approached him.

"Hey Noah," I said.

"Hi-," he began when he was rudely interrupted.

"Noah, babe c'mon," Jackie said.

"Could you give us a moment?" I asked her.

"No, I can't," she stated. I rolled my eyes and went to speak when she poured her water bottle all over me. I jumped and felt the blouse of my uniform clinging to my body.

"Jackie!" Noah said, and I glared at her.

"Aria!" Christina's voice pulled me out of my irrational thoughts. She took me by the arm to the restroom.

"Are you alright?" she asked.

"Yeah, just a little damp. Again."

"Let's go talk to the Dean," she said.

"No, it's fine," I shrugged.

"She can't do this and not get punished," Christina said.

"It's okay. It was just water," I replied. The last thing I wanted was a repeat of what I've gone through in the past. We walked out of the bathroom and she frowned at me. "Let's just get to class," I said knowing that what happened in the lunch room was nothing.

By the end of the day, I didn't even bother waiting for Noah. I walked down the street and before I could turn to walk onto my road, a familiar motorcycle pulled up next to me.

"Ditching me?" he asked.

"I'll probably get a pumpkin spice latte thrown at me tomorrow if I get on that bike," I commented.

"Well, I'm not gonna let that happen. Climb on," he said and held out the extra helmet to me. I smiled, took it, and climbed on the bike.

We got to Noah's house and both worked on our respective papers. I sat on the loveseat adjacent to the long sofa where we had sat the previous night.

"How're you doing?" he asked.

"About a page in. You?"

"Same," he sighed and looked at me.

"Wanna listen to some music?" he asked. I nodded and sat down my laptop while he scrolled through his phone and connected it to a speaker in a bookcase by the window. I stood up to stretch and Noah turned around as some slow music played through the living room.

"This is what Noah Turner listens to when he's alone?" I laughed lightly. He rolled his eyes and shook his head lightly.

"I'm not alone," he pointed out. Noah watched as I looked around the living room trying to avoid his gaze. "Are you hungry?" he asked.

"Yeah," I responded and followed him into the kitchen. He opened a cupboard and pulled out a box of noodles.

"Spaghetti sound okay?" he asked. I suddenly got uncomfortable.

"Oh, you don't have to make something like that," I said.

"That's alright, my dad can have some when he gets home too," he shrugged. I couldn't help but watch his muscles flex under his shirt as he reached the top shelf to pull down the jar of sauce.

"You and your dad get along?" I asked as I sat at the island across from the stove he was working on.

"Eh, sometimes," Noah answered.

"And your mom?" I asked. Noah's head dropped, and he shook it a moment later.

"She passed away last year," he shared.

"Oh. Oh, I am so sorry," I said quickly.

"It's fine. We had been expecting it. Three years ago, she was diagnosed with stage four colon cancer. It was relentless," he said as the water on the stove began to boil. He poured the box of noodles into the pan and turned around to look at me.

"You're very strong. Your mom would be proud," I said. Noah smiled at me and stirred the noodles.

"Well, lucky for you, she taught me how to cook," he said, lightening the mood.

"I can't wait," I smiled.

While Noah cooked, I brought my laptop to the kitchen to keep him company while I finished my paper. Once I hit save, Noah slid a plate in front of me and I shut my laptop.

"Coke, water, or milk?" he asked and opened the fridge, looking for anything else he may have to offer.

"Milk, please," I replied. He poured us both a glass and joined me at the island. I ate, and he watched me,

"What?" I laughed.

"Is it good?"

"Very," I praised. Noah smiled and dug in himself. I sucked up a noodle and it hit my cheek making Noah and me laugh. He used his thumb and wiped off the sauce on my cheek making me tense up. *Oh... okay*. I was blushing. I know I was. I looked away and we sat in silence for a moment, until the front door opened.

"Noah?" I heard his father's voice. I could have sworn the color drained from Noah's face.

"Dad? You're home early," Noah said.

"Aren't you supposed to be at practice?" he asked sternly.

"I-It, uh, was canceled," Noah fumbled.

"Take her home," his dad stated. Noah went to protest when his father shook his head, "NOW!" he barked. Noah and I both jumped as his father disappeared off down the hall.

"I'll grab my things," I said quietly. Noah nodded as I slid around the corner and collected my bag from the living room. I came back into the kitchen and he held his keys in his hand and already had on his leather jacket.

When we pulled up in the driveway, my dad was climbing out of his car.

"Thanks for dinner," I said to Noah as I climbed off the bike.

He nodded silently, and I turned to join my dad on the sidewalk.

"Who's that?" he asked as we walked inside.

"Noah Turner," I shared.

"Does your mother know about this?" he asked as we entered the kitchen.

"About what? That I am tutoring him? Yes," I said.

"That's all that is going on?" he asked.

"Yes, Dad," I sighed and walked off to my room.

Lying in bed, my mind kept drifting to the evening with Noah. Talking about his mother... dinner... I was catching feelings for him, but I couldn't bring myself to do anything about it. Especially not with Jackie.

I walked into school the next morning and Christina ran down the hallway toward me.

"Woah, where's the fire?" I joked.

"You won't believe this!" she gushed attempting to catch her breath.

"What?" I laughed.

"Noah dumped Jackie last night," she said. My eyes widened,

"What?"

"Right! I guess he drove over and broke things off! That's what I am hearing," she said. I looked over at my locker noticing Noah wasn't here.

"Have you seen either of them?"

"Jackie's here and she's PISSED. I haven't seen Noah," she shrugged. I nodded and walked over to my locker. When I opened it, eggs came falling out and cracked around my feet. I frowned and looked up to see people laughing. But one group of people watching caught my eye. Jackie and her "squad".

The day went by and Noah didn't show up at all. I considered texting him but didn't want to be weird. As I walked home, I couldn't help but text him.

"You okay?"

After I hit send, I wanted to take it back immediately. I put my phone away as I walked home. I didn't have any homework tonight, so I moved things around my room. Maybe the bed would look better by the window?

Seven o'clock rolled around and my phone lit up,

Noah: Sorry I took so long to respond. I was at practice.

I furrowed my eyebrows.

"You weren't at classes today,"

I sent back. I waited, and a message appeared.

"I know. You mind filling me in?"

I smiled to myself and sent back,

"I'll come over now,"

I collected my things and made copies of my notes, stapling them in a nice packet before slipping it in my folder and calling a cab.

Once I stood outside Noah's front door, my phone buzzed,

"Don't worry about it, I'll see you tomorrow."

I froze and went to turn around when the front door opened.

"Oh, Mr. Turner, hi... I-."

"May I help you?" he asked.

"I, um, I'm here to see Noah," I said. His father was ready to respond when I heard Noah.

"Who is it?" he asked. I looked around Noah's dad to see him with a huge bruise across his cheek.

"Oh my god, are you okay?" I asked Noah. His father walked away leaving us at the door.

"I'm fine. Had an accident at football practice," he said.

"I... I, um, brought you notes for what you missed today," I said and reached into my bag to pull out the papers I stapled together for him. He took them and smiled at me.

"Thanks Aria," he said.

"Of course," I responded.

"I'll drive you home," he said.

"No, don't worry about it," I shrugged but he didn't listen as he grabbed his keys and my wrist.

Once Noah was parked in my driveway, I climbed off the bike and noticed he looked completely zoned out.

"Are you really okay?" I asked. Noah looked up at me through his eyelashes. "Your dad hit you, didn't he?" Noah nodded, and I stared at him. "Because of me?" I added.

"What? No, Aria it's not because of you. It's because I skipped practice," he said.

"Because you were with me instead," I pointed out.

"And that was my choice. It was not because of you," he said. I looked at him and he turned to face me. "I'll see you tomorrow morning," he said, and I stepped back, watching as he left.

When I descended the staircase the next morning, my parents sat together in the dining room.

"Aria?" I heard my mom's voice.

"Yeah?"

"Could you come in here? We'd like to talk."

I joined my parents and my mom sighed.

"Your father and I have been discussing this the last day or so and we want to express our worries with you."

"Worries?" I asked.

"This Noah guy... the last few days you've been running off to see him," My dad began.

"And?" I asked growing confused and agitated.

"We're afraid this is going to be a repeat of what happened in Wisconsin, Aria."

My mind flashed back to the laughter and tears.

"We're afraid he's going to turn on you," my mom added.

"No, I really don't think he's like that," I said.

"We don't want to believe so, but he doesn't have a good reputation, Aria. Neither does his dad," my dad revealed.

"What do you mean?" I asked.

"Noah was a father for nearly a month before his son died. It was a premature birth. He has been known to mess with girls and that's the last thing you need," my dad stated. My heart was racing. He was a dad? Noah had a son? With who? Was he a player?

"Okay. Look, I need to get to school. I'll keep everything you've said in mind," I said as I made my way out.

Noah stood at his locker speaking to Cadin.

"Aria, just the beauty I was looking for," Cadin said.

"Pardon?" I asked and even Noah gave Cadin his full attention.

"I was wondering if you'd like to catch a movie tonight?" Cadin asked. Suddenly, it felt like my heart was beating in my throat.

"Oh, I, um-."

"Cadin," Noah said and looked sternly at his friend.

"What?" Cadin smiled at him. Noah's face was cold as stone while he shut his locker and looked at me.

"Head to class," Noah said. I glanced at both of them in confusion before sliding through the halls to class.

Noah came in not long after and all through class I kept wanting to ask him what the attitude with Cadin was about, and about his kid, but I couldn't bring *that* up. Mrs. Milton came around the room to each of us and went over our rough drafts we had to submit online. She checked over mine and said I was heading in a wonderful direction. However, when she got to Noah, she frowned.

"Mr. Turner, this isn't finished," she sighed. I looked at the back of Noah's head and he looked down.

"I know. I apologize, it will get finished. I actually have a tutoring session with Miss Boyd tonight," Noah began and turned to face me. "Right?"

"Yep," I lied.

"Wonderful. I'm glad you're reaching out for help. If you need anything don't be afraid to contact me as well," she said before moving onto the next student.

I stopped at my locker before lunch and noticed Noah at his, talking to a girl from my Algebra II class. She giggled, and I slid behind him to open my locker.

"My dad's not back till late if you wanna stop by after the game? I'd happily give you a ride," he said. I couldn't help but roll my eyes. I switched out my books before heading into the lunchroom.

"Aria!"

I looked up to see Cadin in front of me.

"Hi," I said.

"Since Turner isn't here... how about that movie?" he asked. I laughed lightly and nodded.

"You know what, why not?" I smiled, and he pulled out his phone to get my number and address.

"Great. I'll see you tonight. There're a few movies that start at seven. We can pick then?"

"Works for me."

"See ya at 6:30."

"Okay," I responded.

Cadin chose a comedy flick and we wound up laughing quite a bit. At the end, we both split up to use the restroom. I turned my phone on to see it blew up,

Noah: "I'm gonna be over after practice?"

"Aria?"

"Are you okay?"

I rolled my eyes as another message came through.

"Do I need to come over?"

I sighed and called him. He answered before a full ring could finish.

"Hey, where are you?" Noah asked.

"What's it to you?"

"I thought you were helping with my paper?" he asked.

"You never actually asked me, Noah. I do have a life," I commented.

"What're you doing?" he asked.

"I'm at the movie theater."

"What?" he spat.

"Look, I went to a movie, is it a big deal?"

"With Cadin?"

"Yes."

"Don't leave the building. I'm coming."

"What? Why?" I waited for a response, but the disconnected dial tone came back at me. "Noah?" I began to panic as I hung up and used the restroom as I had planned. I washed my hands and stepped out of the restroom to see Cadin waiting for me across the hall.

"You okay?" he asked as I approached him.

"Yeah, my grandma called, sorry," I lied.

"That's fine. Are you ready to go?"

In the back of my mind red flags were flying.

"We could go into the arcade?" I suggested motioning to the separate section of the theater with pinball, air hockey, and a pool table.

"Um, yeah... sure," he said. His mood changed from the smiley guy I was spending time with at school to suddenly very abrupt and bothered. I walked over and pulled a dollar out of my pocket approaching the counter to get tokens for a game. After taking the balls and rack, I began setting the table up as Cadin took the cues. I started to line myself up and felt Cadin press himself up behind me.

"What're you doing?" I began nervously, but quickly giggled to cover it and seem flirty.

"Hm? Nothing, just thinking maybe we should get out of here?" he whispered in my ear. My eyes widened, and I bent back down.

"After this game," I said. Cadin didn't get into it at all. He was uptight, and I noticed he was trying to sink the 8 ball.

After winning, I looked around for Noah. Where was he? Cadin returned everything to the counter and he motioned for me to walk with him. I couldn't come up with another excuse.

"We could play again?" I tried as he took my arm firmly.

"It's getting late. I should get you home."

"It's only 9:30," I responded.

"Some time to enjoy ourselves then," he said quietly. We got out in the parking lot and I dug my heels into the ground, breaking his grip.

"Cadin, stop! What the hell!" I shouted.

"Aria, I'm taking you home."

"Are you? Why are you acting so weird, hm? I don't want to have sex with you!"

"That's not what I was trying to do. Sorry, but I don't think my dick could handle all your weight," Cadin remarked. My mouth fell open and Cadin went to grip my wrist again when I pushed him down and his body slapped the pavement. He stood up and reached for me again but before he could, he was knocked back down. I looked next to me and saw Noah straighten up.

"Turner!" Cadin groaned as he sat up and wiped some of the blood that fell from his nose off.

"Fuck off, Cadin!"

"Well, of course you want her all to yourself. Gotta get with every girl in the school," he spat as he stood up.

"What?" Noah growled.

"You heard me!" Cadin shouted back as Noah used his broad shoulders and lunged at Cadin knocking him harshly against the concrete again and I jumped.

"Noah! Noah, get off him!" I yelled. He went to punch Cadin when I grabbed his shoulder and he froze, looking over his shoulder at me. Cadin used that opportunity to slide out from beneath him and run.

Noah stood, and I ran my fingers through my hair.

"I didn't think you were showing up."

"Traffic was bad."

"That's all you have to say?"

"Oh, right. I told you so," he added.

"Excuse me?" I snapped.

"I told you not to go out with him."

"No, you didn't!"

"Well I thought my hint was enough," he shrugged. I shook my head as Noah began walking away.

"Woah, wait. Where are you going?" I asked.

"Home."

I crossed my arms over my chest and popped my hip out as he stood still watching me.

"Oh, do you need a ride?" he asked tauntingly.

"Screw you, Noah," I sighed feeling defeated.

"I think you mean thank you," he said as he motioned for me to walk with him back to his bike.

Noah's motorcycle pulled into the driveway once again and I handed him back his helmet.

"There you are," he said. I looked at him and admired the deep dimple in his cheeks as he formed a thin line with his lips.

"Aria!"

I turned to see my mom standing outside on the front porch, arms across her chest. She watched me get into Cadin's car earlier, so she surely will have questions.

"You're being summoned," Noah said breaking me out of

thought.

"Yeah." I sighed and looked at him. "Thank you. Tonight, could've ended a lot worse," I said. He nodded and shrugged lightly.

"It's over now. Will I see you at the game tomorrow?"

"I don't know. Gotta see what happens tonight first."

"Right. Well, goodnight Aria, I'll see you in the morning."

"Night," I responded and walked up to the house.

"Again?" my mom scolded once the front door shut behind the both of us. "Where's the boy from earlier?"

"He tried to date rape me," I summarized. My dad stood up from his armchair in the living room and joined us in the walk-way.

"Excuse me?"

"Cadin. I called Noah and he came to get me," I lied.

"You didn't bother to call the police, or one of us?"

"I didn't want to cause a big deal..."

"This is a big deal, Aria!" my mom shouted. I sighed and shook my head.

"May I please just go to bed?"

"Yes," my dad answered.

When I walked in the building the next morning, whispers were all I heard. As I approached my locker, Noah was mid-make out with a girl I didn't recognize. I collected my things and made my way to Mrs. Milton's room. I took my seat and waited as Noah came in. He didn't look in my direction and I frowned. I was hoping maybe he knew what was going on. I tapped his shoulder, but he completely ignored me. I reached forward to try again and Mrs. Milton began her lecture.

Noah made it out of the classroom before I could catch him. While I walked down the hall, people would glance at me and resume their conversations.

"Aria?"

Finally, a familiar voice.

"Hey, Christina. What the hell is going on?" I asked. She pulled me into the restroom and peeked under all the stalls.

"The football team made a bet that Cadin wouldn't be able to get in your pants-."

"What!"

"I know. But don't feel bad, Cadin is cute so I wouldn't blame-."

"Woah, no! You actually believe that happened?"

"It didn't? Everyone was saying it did!" she said shocked.

"No! No, it didn't! That lying piece of shit!" I spat. Wait, the football team... Noah?

"I'm so sorry. I thought you were embarrassed," Christina sighed. I shook my head and felt tears in my eyes.

"Oh, no, no, don't cry! How about we hang out tonight? Go to the mall? I'll drive you home and meet your parents?" Christina asked.

"Yeah, sure. That sounds great," I smiled as she opened her arms and hugged me. What do I do about the football team?

Only two hours into walking through the mall did we final decide to hit the food court. We sat down and began digging in when my phone went off.

Noah Turner: INCOMING CALL

"Who's that?" Christina asked. I hit ignore and shrugged.

"Wrong number," I lied. Not even a minute later, he called

back.

"Doesn't sound like a wrong number," she commented. I hit accept and she looked at the caller ID as she slid in the seat next to me.

"Hey," I answered.

"Hey. Look, I am sorry I ignored you today. There's a lot going on with the team-."

"Like making bets?" I shot back.

"I didn't want it to happen-."

"Oh, really?"

"I was there to make sure nothing happened. I tried to warn you!"

"Wow, you're such an asshole," I laughed bitterly. Christina listened intently as Noah took a moment.

"Are you coming to the game tonight?"

"No."

"I really want to see you," he said. The slight crack in his voice made me ponder for a moment, but my wall still stood.

"I don't care," I replied and hung up. Christina looked at me with wide eyes.

"Noah Turner just called you to apologize? What?" she asked.

"Yeah... I don't know," I sighed realizing she didn't have a clue about all my secret meetings with Noah. Well, technically nobody but our parents knew.

"Hey... Don't listen to them. You are so beautiful, they obviously wish they could have you. You can't let them believe they got to you. Let's go to the game. It's your turn to ignore Noah."

Our team was winning 24-7 and Noah's name was constantly heard over the loudspeaker. Before we knew it, halftime came around and Noah was looking around the stadium. When his eyes landed on me, he started to make his way over until the coach stopped him. He looked at me and once the coach was done, a teammate grabbed his attention. They noticed me and Cadin looked over. I could tell words were being exchanged and I heard someone say,

"Noah, you gettin' it with Cadin's sloppy seconds?"

Laughter filled the sidelines until Noah tackled down the player who made the comment. Christina grabbed my arm and I noticed Noah's dad came running down from the stands. I watched as his father had a firm grip on the back of his neck and he hit his father's arm off him as he walked back up to the locker room.

Christina and I watched the rest of the game. We ended up losing and as we left the stadium, I noticed Noah sat on his motor-cycle wearing a hoodie and sweatpants.

"Aria!" he called. I looked at Christina and she eyed me.

"I'll be right back," I said to her. I walked over and noticed Noah busted his lip open.

"Aria, I'm sorry."

"Why'd they say that to you?" I asked.

"I… I defended you in the locker room before the game. They thought I was just being funny," he said and shook his head.

"Oh."

"I really am sorry. You don't deserve this," he apologized again. I nodded and looked at Christina.

"Let's go. I wanna take you somewhere," he said. I looked at him cautiously. "Just a diner about fifteen minutes away. Won't risk running into anyone."

I turned to Christina and nodded,

"Go ahead, Noah's taking me home," I lied. She nodded and gave me a quick hug before I joined Noah on the bike and put on the helmet.

We pulled up outside Rex's Diner and Noah walked us in and sat at a booth in the back. An older woman approached and asked if we wanted anything. Noah said no, but I asked for coffee.

"Why are we here?" I asked after she returned with my mug and a small dish of creamer. I dumped one in and grabbed three packets of sugar.

"I just want to talk to you. This school is small," he began, and I took a sip of the coffee. "You're not a cheerleader. If I talk to you-."

"It ruins your reputation. I get it."

"It's not that. People are ruthless and think it's funny to poke fun at those who are "easy targets" ... and I am one of those people," he shrugged.

I snickered, "You? Noah, I've seen you kick people's ass."

"I'm a little hot-headed, yes. But that's not a good thing," he pointed out.

"Okay... so change."

"It's not that easy, Aria," he stated. I rolled my eyes and he watched me carefully.

"You brought me here for that?"

"I like talking to you. I enjoy your company. I think we could be great friends. But for the sake of our social lives... I just think we need to hang out... under the radar," he suggested. I nodded and took another sip.

"What happened at the game?"

"Which part?" he commented.

"The coach, your dad?"

"Oh... I'm... uh, suspended for the next game... And dad is pissed," he shrugged. I nodded, and his attention turned to the song playing through the speakers. "Hungry Eyes" from *Dirty Dancing* played, and Noah started to sing. My hands flew to my mouth to cover the giggles that were threatening to escape,

"What?" he laughed.

"Bravo," I teased.

"It's a jam," he shrugged.

"Okay, Noah," I laughed as I finished my coffee.

"Ready to go?" he asked. I nodded as he pulled out his wallet and put down a five.

October

A month passed, and the big topic was homecoming. I stood at my locker and grabbed my things as Christina found me.

"Spotting any potential homecoming dates?" she asked. I laughed lightly and shook my head.

"Not really. I don't think I'm gonna go," I shrugged.

"What? No! You have to go," she frowned.

"I have next year," I pointed out.

"It's not the same," she commented. I sighed, and she started to pout.

"Fine. I'll go."

"Yay!" She squealed and reached into her planner. "Cause I already got you a ticket."

"What? Christina!"

"They were cheaper in couples," she shrugged. I laughed lightly as Noah approached his locker.

"Morning Noah," Christina said. He glanced at her and nodded briefly.

"Oh-Kay," she commented, and we split up walking to our classes.

I jumped lightly as a folded paper fell on my desk after Noah stretched. I unfolded the paper to read,

"You going to homecoming?"

I grabbed my pencil and wrote,

"Yep."

I handed it back to him and he read it before returning the paper.

"With?"

I smirked and wrote,

"Who says I have to go with anyone?"

I tapped his arm with the corner of the paper, and he took it. Noah peeked over his shoulder at me with a smirk and nodded lightly.

"It's cute," Christina said as I spun around and looked at the dress in the mirror.

"I really like it," I admitted.

"It hugs your curves perfectly," she agreed. Then I panicked.

"It does?"

"In a good way. Aria, calm down," she laughed.

"Are you sure?"

"Yeah. Do you want to try others on?" she asked, and I looked at myself again. With makeup and my hair done, I'd feel like a different person.

"No, this is the one," I confirmed.

"Ladies."

I turned to see Noah behind Christina.

"Noah, what're you doing here?" Christina asked.

"Ah, my date is looking at dresses," he said. I looked across the store to see a skinny girl in a cheer uniform from another school. How many girls does he know? I quickly kicked that thought from my mind. We had been hanging out a bit here and there over the last month, and he never mentioned who he was bringing to the dance.

"She looks like Michael Jackson... One too many nose jobs?" Christina laughed.

"Christina!" I scolded.

"Ha... she's, um, different," Noah laughed lightly, and I backed off. "I'll see you both Saturday night?" he said and returned to her after giving us a small wave. I looked back in the mirror and Christina looked at me.

"Is there something going on with you two?" Christina asked.

"Hm? No, why?" I asked and scrunched my nose.

"I don't know. He just seems... different," she shrugged.

"You know him better than I do," I replied and returned to the changing room.

Saturday night came quickly. Christina showed up at my house and my parents made us take photos together before heading off to the school. We walked into our gymnasium and there were lights strung around.

"I'll grab some punch," Christina said as I stood by a table and chairs. I looked around and spotted my lab partner, Cadin and his date, then Noah and his date.

"Aria?"

I turned to see a guy with a yellow button up, suspenders, and corduroy pants. His glasses were beginning to slide down the bridge of his nose as he spoke.

"Would you like to dance?" he asked. I looked around and nodded.

"Yeah, sure," I said kindly.

"Oh. Really? I've never gotten this far," he said quietly.

"Sure," I repeated as I put my arms around his neck. He carefully placed his hands on my waist and smiled showing his braces.

"I'm Dicky," he said as I swayed with him.

"Nice to meet you, Dicky," I said.

"You're the first person who has ever danced with me," he shared.

"Oh," I commented and looked around to see Noah, Cadin, and other football players looking in my direction. They were all laughing. Well, all except Noah.

The song ended, and I said goodbye to Dicky before finding Christina with my punch.

"Did you just dance with Icky Dicky?" she asked.

"Uh… yeah. Is that bad?" I asked.

"No… I mean, he's just a total nerd. Not a big deal, that was nice of you," she said, and I frowned as I took a sip of my drink and looked over at Noah who was already looking at me. I noticed my black dress matched his black tie… as his dates dress was black as well, but still… I couldn't help picturing myself next to him tonight. Jackie appeared and began talking to Noah. His date walked off to leave them be and it didn't take long for them to start arguing. Jackie stormed off to the dance floor and Noah stormed into the hallway, looking agitated.

"I'll be back. Gotta use the restroom," I said and slid between sweaty bodies to the doors that lead to the hallway. I walked down and turned the corner to see Noah with his back to a set of lockers, leaning with his hands on his face.

"Noah?" I asked. He looked up at me and straightened up.

"Yeah," he said.

"Are you okay?"

"I'm fine. How was your dance with Dicky?" he asked, a smirk on his face.

"Extremely awkward. He's never danced with anyone," I frowned. He smiled at me and I watched as he looked down the hall.

"That was sweet of you," he added. I nodded, and he looked me over slowly. "You look beautiful," he said.

"Oh... thanks," I smiled, and he grinned in return. Both of us could still hear the music in the gym and I laughed when I realized "Hungry Eyes" was playing.

"What're the odds of that?" Noah asked. I smiled up at him and froze as his hand cupped my cheek and he leaned down, pressing his lips to mine. It was a lingering kiss that had me frozen in place. I didn't know what to do. I had never been kissed! Noah pulled back slowly and frowned. "I shouldn't have..." he shook his head and almost seemed flustered. "Aria, say something," he added.

"Wow," escaped my lips and Noah let out a small sigh that turned into a laugh. "Why?" I asked, and Noah shook his head.

"It felt right," he said. I nodded, and he stood up straighter. "We should get back," he added. I nodded and walked back in while Noah waited in the hall.

"You okay?" Christina asked when I returned.

"Yeah, I kinda spaced out."

"Uh," Christina began. I turned, and Noah was approaching me.

"Would you like to dance?" he asked.

"What?" I jumped.

"My date is dancing with someone, thought I'd ask you," he shrugged. Christina eyed him, and I nodded. He took my hand and I felt his hands move to my waist once we stood in the group of people.

"What are you doing?" I whispered to him.

"Don't get mad-."

"Noah," I glared at him.

"I'm trying to not make people suspicious, okay? And I wanted to dance with you."

"Okay?" I asked when his hand came down on my ass.

"Noah!" I yelled and pushed him away. I looked over and several guys were laughing. He looked at me with worried eyes and I stomped over to Christina.

"What the hell!" she remarked standing up.

"I think it's time to go," I said.

"Yeah, let's go," she said and led me out. Was the kiss for his friends too? I felt betrayed, but I didn't want to believe that he was doing it for his friends.

I showered and changed from my dress into a tank top and sweatpants when something hit my window. I opened it and looked down to see Noah.

"What're you doing?" I whisper-yelled at him.

"Let me in."

"No!"

"Please?"

I looked behind me and motioned for him to walk around the house. I snuck downstairs and looked at him.

"I'm sor-," I stopped him and put my hand over his mouth before shutting the front door behind me and moving away from the door.

"What are you doing here?" I asked. It was hard to argue with him when he still had on his nice button up from the dance.

"You know why I did that-."

"Okay, but you kissed me! Was that for them too?"

"No, Aria... that was 100% me. I... I enjoy being around you. You're not like everyone else," he said and slid his arms around my waist.

"I'm not as great as you think."

"You're amazing," he smiled. I grinned up at him and he looked at his bike in the driveway.

"I'm gonna get going. How about I bring you over after school tomorrow?"

"Yeah, sounds great," I smiled.

"Night, Aria," he said and kissed my forehead.

Noah and I plopped down on the sofa together after school on Monday. He threw on some TV show where friends pranked each other, and his arm fell around me.

"Oh, no, no, no!" I said, and Noah looked at me in confusion, moving his arm.

"What?"

"You're not pulling the whole "make a move" on me thing. Nope."

"Oh, come on! Girls love cuddling!" he commented.

"D-Did Noah Turner just ask to cuddle?" I laughed. Noah rolled his eyes and smirked. "Oh... He did!" I teased as he leaned forward and pecked my lips. I grinned, and Noah kissed me again, our lips attaching every few seconds until I felt his tongue press against my lips. In shock, my mouth fell open, Noah taking full advantage of the moment, holding me in his arms as he fell on top of me and pushed me against the cushions. I giggled, and he smirked into the kiss when we both heard the front door open and close.

"Noah Francis Turner!"

Noah sat up and I followed to see his dad getting closer. Noah jumped up and put his hands out before him. I couldn't believe how vulnerable he was.

"Dad, breathe," Noah said quickly and carefully before his

dad gripped my arm and lifted me from the couch.

"Ow!" I glared.

"Don't touch her!" Noah yelled, and I tried to free myself from his dad's grip. Mr. Turner's grasp tightened and then loosened, the combination of me pulling and him letting me go causing me to stumble into Noah. Noah put his arm around my shoulders to steady me.

Pointing toward the front door, he looked at me and Noah and screamed, "Get out! Both of you!"

"I don't know how the hell he keeps getting off work early," Noah spat as he pulled in the driveway. I climbed off the bike and looked at him.

"If he hadn't shown up… was it heading… further?" I asked. Noah studied my face for a moment.

"If you wanted it to," he responded. I stayed silent as Noah's eyes were glued to me.

"Can I ask you something?" I blurted.

"Sure."

"Were you a father?" I asked. Noah sighed and looked down.

"Yeah, I was," he replied.

"Oh."

"It's over though, I've put everything behind me."

"Who were you with?" He watched me for a moment and pursed his lips.

"Francesca."

I thought for a moment and realized I didn't know who it was off the top of my head.

"Oh… Thanks for telling me."

"Why would I lie about it?" he asked. I shrugged, and he smiled. "I'm also clean if that's what you're worried about."

"No, no... I'm not," I said quickly. God, I wasn't even thinking about sleeping with him.

"Okay?" Noah laughed nervously and watched me carefully.

"My parents heard and they just... don't trust you," I shared.

"I get it," he said. I nodded, and he looked up at the house. "I'll see you tomorrow," he said.

"Wait- what about your dad?"

"Just gotta give him time to cool off," Noah answered.

"Okay, I'll see you tomorrow."

"Bye Aria, goodnight," he said and drove off.

As I laid in bed that night, my mind kept wandering to Noah. I couldn't help but wonder what this relationship was to him. Am I just another girl? Or someone he can see a future with? What if I end up pregnant? Will he want me to keep it? I know I want the father of my children to stick around. I will not raise a broken family. That's not what I want. I'm already way ahead of myself. I don't want to push him away with these thoughts so soon.

The end of the school day came around and when I opened my locker, a note fell out.

"Aria" was scribbled in Noah's small yet clear handwriting.

"7 o'clock. Park behind your house."

I smirked and looked around the hallway to see Noah leaning against one of his friend's lockers sending a wink in my direction. I walked home and worked on my school work as I heard my mom cooking in the kitchen downstairs. I ran down and she looked at me.

"How was school?" she asked.

"Good, boring," I replied, and she nodded. "I'm meeting Christina at the park around seven," I added.

"Okay, I'll save you some food," my mom smiled.

"Sounds like a plan."

I sat on the swings for a few minutes when I heard Noah's bike pull up. I ran over, and he already had the helmet held out to me. My eyes landed on the blanket and picnic basket attached on the back of the bike but didn't say anything as I climbed on.

About ten minutes outside town Noah pulled down a narrow dirt trail in the middle of a forest.

"Um, where are we going?" I asked.

"Sh, it's a secret," he responded. I stayed quiet as we pulled up to an old shack by a large pond. The pier was worn and broke in the middle. Noah parked his bike, grabbed the blanket off the back of his bike and motioned to the deck as he walked over and spread the blanket.

"Does this belong to someone?" I asked.

"It's old and worn, doubt anyone's been out here," he shrugged and stood next to me, taking the basket and returning to the blanket where he laid down and smiled up at me. "Care to join me?" he grinned and pulled out several candles. I sat down and watched as Noah put the match box down when he was done.

He pulled out two sandwich bags containing a pita of some sort and two small mason jars with what looked like cheesecake inside. He fished out a bottle of water and handed me a lemonade before saying,

"My mom taught me how to make these as well."

"What is it?" I asked curiously as I opened the bag.

"A Mediterranean chicken salad sandwich," he smiled.

"Okay, and the jar?"

"Key lime and blueberry pie... just in a jar for easy travel," he smirked.

"I'm impressed."

"Yeah? The lemonade is Minute Maid, though," he said quickly to include his tiny disclaimer.

"This is really nice Noah," I responded.

"I'm glad you like it."

We began eating and Noah reached into the basket again and pulled out a Canon EOS Rebel camera and snapped a photo while I ate.

"Noah!" I exclaimed and hid my face.

"What?" he laughed and looked down at the screen. We stayed silent for a minute until he looked up at me through his eyebrows.

"I've been thinking about joining the school paper," I said as I ate.

"Really?"

"Yeah, it'd be good practice."

"Journalist, Aria Boyd," he said and lifted his camera again.

"With photography by Noah Turner," I commented. Noah's eyed popped up and I could see a light bulb turn on.

"We should do the paper together."

"You think?" I asked.

"Yeah, more of an excuse to see each other, not as much sneaking..."

"Okay... yeah."

"The advisor is Mrs. Todd, she teaches freshman English."

"I'll stop in after school tomorrow," I said.

"Me too, I'll be able to show up more after football season is over. But then I start a community league. Luckily those practices aren't until later at night."

"Cool."

"I expect to see you there," he winked.

"You know I will."

"You two would like to join?" Mrs. Todd asked us as we stood in the doorway of the newspaper classroom.

"Yes. We brought some of our work," I smiled holding up a folder as Noah held up his camera.

"Let's take a look," she said and led us to her desk where she had two chairs beside it. We sat down, and Noah allowed her to flip through his camera. She nodded and then stopped at a photo and smiled,

"I like this one," she said and turned it, showing a photo of me eating my chicken salad last night. I blushed, and Noah smiled lightly.

"Okay, and you Aria?" she asked as I handed over my folder. She opened it and read through my first article, "What Really Happens in the Kitchen". I wrote it when a friend of mine from my last school worked as a waitress part time. She skimmed a few others and nodded.

"We meet after school every day. I only require at least once a week and that is for your turn-in day. An article a week, or one hundred photos a week in your case," she started and looked at Noah. "Photos of any sort, we can let yearbook use as well, so the more the better. Noah, we were actually looking to interview you, the quarterback and being your senior year..." she shrugged and looked at me. "Aria, would you like to do it?" Mrs. Todd asked. I looked over at Noah and he smiled.

"Um, yeah. Sure thing," I responded.

"Wonderful! I'll leave you off to do whatever you have planned. Dicky over there has sports photos on his computer if you'd like to find any of Noah, I'm sure we have plenty," she commented eyeing some of the girls in the room. I looked around and noticed most of them I haven't really seen or met. Then it dawned on me, this class is a freshman through senior club, so they were probably younger.

Noah and I stood up and slid his camera strap around his neck as I followed him out of the classroom into the hallway.

"I need to get to practice, I'm already late. You wanna go? You can use my camera and get your own shots," he said.

"Will you give me a ride?"

"Of course. We could even head down to that diner?" he asked and slid his hands to my waist, pulling me close.

"I don't have any money."

"Don't be silly."

"Noah, you don't need to buy me food."

"The boyfriend pays," he jokingly argued.

"Boyfriend?" I asked. Noah got quiet and put his head down.

"Yeah?" he asked shyly.

"No… I mean, yeah. I just… didn't expect to hear you say it, I don't know," I said.

"I'll see you in a little bit, okay?" he asked and smiled as he took the camera from around his neck and put it around mine.

"Okay," I said, and Noah pecked my forehead.

I used the restroom before walking down the street to the field. I could hear the coaches whistle from the field as I descended the stadium steps. My heart nearly stopped as my eyes landed on a shirtless Noah Turner. Isn't that… against school policy or something? I felt my cheeks getting warm as I turned on his camera. A few of the players noticed me, but once they saw the camera they went back to focusing on practice. My nerves wore off as I took my photos of a few of the players, trying subconsciously not to take too many of Noah. At least until he puts his jersey back on.

"Did you get some good shots?" Noah asked as we sat in our booth and ordered dinner at Rex's Diner.

"I guess..." I responded as I handed Noah back his camera.

"Let's see," he began as he turned on the camera and flipped through. "Aria, these photos look amazing," Noah smiled.

"Thanks," I said brushing his comment off.

"No, I'm serious. Like this one," he said and turned the camera, so I could see a photo of Matt, one of the wide receivers. "The angle is great, you caught Matt mid-pass. That's worth a spot in the yearbook for sure," he said as he continued flipping through a few more. I noticed Noah's eyebrows furrow as he reached a few of my other photos.

"Um, you're not using these... are you?" Noah asked and quirked an eyebrow at me as he turned the camera showing a few shots of him without his shirt on. "Or are these for your own personal collection?" Noah smirked and winked at me. Our waitress came over with our food and Noah sat down his camera before diving into his fries. "There's a party coming up..." he began. I looked up at him and nodded.

"Matt's Halloween party, right?" I asked.

"Yeah. Are you going?"

"Parties aren't really my thing, Noah."

"I know... but you can still go...I want you there," he said.

"I don't have a costume," I said coming up with an excuse.

"We can go look! How about tomorrow?" he asked as he picked up his burger and took a big bite. I giggled lightly at the way his nose scrunched.

"I don't know..."

"Please?" he asked with his mouth full.

"We can't even spend time together," I pointed out as he chewed. He held up his finger as he swallowed what he had in his mouth.

"Yes, we can. Just keep an eye on me when we're there."

"I'm sure that won't be hard," I smirked. Noah rose an eyebrow at me and grinned.

"What do you think?" I asked as I held up a maid costume to my chest.

"Oh... my... um, are you serious?" Noah asked rubbing the back of his neck.

"Not at all!" I laughed and put it back. Noah flipped through a few racks and pulled a hanger out. "One of the three musketeers?" I asked.

"No! Prince Charming," he smiled.

"Oh... totally," I laughed and rolled my eyes.

"What? You don't think I can pull it off?" he asked coming up behind me and wrapping his arms around my waist.

"No," I shook my head and stayed silent for a moment as he rested his chin atop my head.

"I think I might have something at home I could put together," I said. Noah stood up straight and through for a second.

"I think I may also, now that you said that."

"Okay. Still wanna look around?" I asked.

"No, I should probably get you home, so I can get back before my dad. Another practice skipped, but I'm not at home already, so hopefully he won't suspect a thing," he said. We walked out, and Noah grabbed my hand before I could climb on the bike.

"Saturday and Sunday night there's a haunted house a town over... we could go together. A little spooky date," he said.

"Spooky date?" I laughed.

"Whatever," he shook his head in embarrassment. "Wanna go?"

"Yeah... I was also thinking, maybe we could tell my parents what's going on between us," I said, and Noah eyed me.

"Really?"

"Yeah, I really like you. You aren't as bad as they think either-."

"Gee, thanks."

"You know what I mean," I said carefully.

"Yeah. Just let me know," he said and kissed my forehead before handing me a helmet.

"I'm so glad you want to go to this party!" Christina smiled as we stood in her room.

"Why not?" I shrugged and finalized my second pigtail.

"It's just around the block, but I'll drive us over. Don't want to walk back when we've been standing all night," she sighed. Christina dressed up as Harley Quinn and I decided to go as Boo from Monsters Inc. It was simple and cute. Noah never told me what his idea was, so I was hoping it wouldn't be like a masquerade.

As we parked along the road, we could see the lights from the backyard and the music wasn't loud until we walked inside. Christina went over to grab drinks and my eyes landed on Satan. Well, the second closest thing. Jackie. She wore a red bra, short skirt, and red fishnet tights with four-inch heels. The horns in her head really gave it away.

"Noah," she began. My eyes moved to Noah who entered from the dining room. He wore a white t-shirt under his typical leather jacket and jeans, but his hair was slicked back. His eyes landed on me and a smile spread across his face.

"Drink," Christina said and handed me a red cup.

"Thanks," I said looking away from Noah.

"Doesn't Jackie look like a slut?" she asked.

"Yeah, just a bit," I responded. My eyes were trained on Noah who was watching me over his cup.

"Wanna dance?" Christina asked.

"Sure," I said, and we walked into the living room where the host, Matt, stood and was talking to Cadin.

"Aw, Aria! Look at you!" Matt said, and I just nodded with a small smile. Only a few songs passed before Christina disappeared to get another drink. I walked into the entryway and Noah came in from the dining room again. He nodded his head upstairs and began to walk, me following not too close behind. He slid into the second room on the left and I joined him as he carefully shut the door.

"Boo, huh?" he asked.

"Yeah, are you just a fancy version of yourself?"

"I was aiming more for Danny from Grease, but I'll take that as a compliment," he responded.

"You still look great."

"And you look adorable," he said. I smiled, and Noah slid his arms around me before kissing me gently. "You've been drinking?" he asked.

"A little. Haven't you?" I asked.

"Water. Last thing I need dad to bitch at me for is drinking," he said.

"Oh."

"I'll drive you home."

"You don't have to. Christina brought me."

"And she's on her- what? Third drink?" he asked and eyed me. I nodded, and he kissed me again. My arms wrapped around his neck when the door opened, and Noah froze as I jumped away from him.

"Oh..." Christina said. A moment passed before it clicked for her. "Ooohhh!" she said, and we shushed her.

"Yeah, I'm driving both of you home," he said and approached Christina. "Keys?" he asked. She reached into her pocket and handed them to him.

Noah drove me home first and we said goodnight as he left to drop off Christina and her car.

The next day, Noah showed up at seven to take me to the haunted house. My mom was in the kitchen and my dad was watching TV, so I announced I was going to a haunted house with Christina and left.

Noah parked in the grass lot and he seemed nervous as he looked around the lot carefully while taking off his helmet.

"Are you okay?" I asked.

"Yeah. Just worried we may see people from school," he said. I nodded my head and he grabbed my hand. "Let's just go and have a good time, yeah?" he asked.

"Yeah," I agreed. He let go of my hand and we climbed off the bike. Noah motioned to the corn maze and looked at me.

"Do you accept the challenge?" he asked me. I rolled my eyes and followed Noah into the maze. After twenty minutes we were exiting the maze.

"That wasn't bad," he said. I smiled up at him admiring the way his dimples only showed when he was giggling mischievously. I noticed a small food trailer selling apple cider and pumpkin chocolate chip cookies. Noah and I got some and sat on a hay bale in the barn behind the trailer. At the other side of the barn they were having hayrides. "Was this fun?" Noah asked.

"Yeah," I said and put my head on his shoulder. He pulled his phone out while we sat, and I looked over at his phone to see it was a message from Jackie. The image attached however, had me jumping up and Noah followed. It was of Christina and Noah kissing in her car.

"What the hell!" I spat. Noah grabbed my wrist with his free hand and sat his cup down on the bale.

"It's not what it looks like, I swear."

"Really?"

"Yes! Have I given you a reason not to trust me?"

"Um, homecoming?" I eyed him.

"Please, let me explain," he sighed. I sat down again and folded my arms across my chest. He moved his cup and sat back down. "She kissed me when I took her home last night. She was pretty drunk. I'm sure she won't even remember," Noah sighed.

"And I'm just supposed to be okay with that? Were you going to tell me?" I asked.

"Yeah, I just didn't know how to bring it up, I didn't want to ruin our date... but that's why I was so skittish when we got here," he said. I shook my head and we sat there while I calmed down.

"Haunted house?" I asked just wanting to move on.

"C'mon," Noah said and stood up. We threw our trash away and he took my hand.

I expected Noah to jump at least once, but every time someone popped out, he just laughed at my reactions. I assumed we were getting toward the end and I started to curl closer to Noah. He put his arm around me as we exited the building and I let out a sigh of relief.

"You didn't jump once!" I complained. Noah smirked and moved his arm from around me to hold my hand again. We walked to his bike and I grabbed my helmet. "I... I'm, uh, telling my parents tonight," I said. Noah tightened the strap on his helmet and looked at me.

"Okay."

"Just be you..." I said, and Noah smiled.

"Don't worry, I'm beyond ready," he said.

"Okay," I said and watched as he climbed on the bike.

Once I walked in the door both of my parents were seated in the living room.

"Motorcycle?" my dad asked and looked at me. I took a deep breath and counted, 1...2...3...

"Noah and I are seeing each other. He'd like to meet you both," I blurted. My dad looked past me to my mom on the sofa and I looked at her.

"Over dinner?" my mom asked. I nodded, and she looked down at the book she had been reading. "Tomorrow night?"

"I'll let him know," I smiled.

"Time to clean the shotgun," my dad sighed and stood up, leaving the room.

I stood in the kitchen the next evening with my mom.

"Where's Dad?" I asked.

"Getting dressed."

"He's changing his clothes?"

"You know he doesn't like Noah," she said.

"He doesn't like what he's heard. He's different," I said. The sound of Noah's motorcycle made me stand up straighter and head for the door. My dad came down the hall and looked out the living room window. He was wearing a plaid button up and khaki pants. Different from his usual t-shirt and jeans. I opened the front door and Noah came up with a bouquet of flowers. He wore a black button-up and jeans. No leather jacket tonight.

"Hey," he smiled at me and handed me the flowers.

"For me?" I asked.

"Of course," he said. I took them into the kitchen and Noah followed close behind me as I pulled out a vase.

"Hello Noah," my mom greeted him.

"Mrs. Boyd," he responded with a smile.

"You can head into the living room, I'll call when the food is ready," she said as I put the flowers in the vase and looked at Noah whose hands slid into his pockets. I led Noah into the living room where my dad sat in the loveseat across from the sofa. Noah sat next to me on the couch and I curled into his side, waiting for his arm to fall around me. Instead, he was rubbing the back of his neck awkwardly.

"Hello, Mr. Boyd," Noah said.

"Noah Turner, right?" my dad asked. Noah nodded, and his lips formed a straight line.

"Yes, Sir."

"Did you two meet at school?"

"Yeah, I ran into him the first day," I answered. Noah cleared his throat,

"We just started seeing each other after homecoming," he added.

"Did you go together?"

"No, I went with Christina," I reminded him. However, my dad wasn't looking for me to answer this one.

"I took a girl from Templeton," Noah answered.

"Girlfriend?" my dad asked.

"No, just someone to go with," Noah shrugged.

"When was your last relationship?"

"Early September. We had been together for two years," Noah answered, and I sat there listening intently, but pretending to focus on the TV.

"And you moved on to my daughter?" my dad asked. Noah sat up a little straighter and cleared his throat again.

"Yes... The feelings were no longer there."

"That's not going to happen again though," my dad said.

"Not a chance," Noah answered evenly. This wasn't going too bad, but dad was pushing his luck with all the questions.

"Dinner!" my mom called. I stood, and Noah walked close behind me as I motioned for him to sit next to me. "What would you like to drink Noah? We have milk, Sprite, Pepsi, apple juice..." my mom trailed off. My dad walked around us and took his usual seat at the table.

"Water is fine, thank you," Noah replied. My mom sat his glass down and we began eating the pork chops, corn casserole, and mashed potatoes she made.

"Oh, wow. I haven't had corn casserole since my mom made it," Noah said.

"Been a while?" my mom asked, and I frowned. I probably should have given my parents some background information.

"Ah, she passed last year," Noah said.

"Oh! What happened?" my mom asked. Even my dad gave Noah his full attention.

"She had colon cancer," Noah said.

"I'm so sorry," my mom said.

"It's alright, she's comfortable now," Noah smiled lightly

and looked at me. I put my head on his shoulder and he laid his on mine for a moment before returning to his meal.

"Are you a junior as well?" my dad asked.

"No, no, I'm a senior," Noah responded between bites.

"So, you're looking at colleges?"

"Oh, yeah."

"What are you going for?" my mom asked.

"I haven't fully decided yet. My dad and I are hoping for a full ride through football," Noah answered. I could tell he wasn't as passionate about the football compared to his photography.

"He takes amazing photographs," I said.

"Really?" my mom asked.

"It's a hobby," Noah shrugged.

"As is football," my dad pointed out. Noah kept quiet and I noticed a slight clench of his jaw out of the corner of my eye.

Noah finished his food before me and my mom began to clean off the dishes.

"Oh, please. Let me," Noah said and cleared the table, taking the dishes into the kitchen. I looked between both of my parents and they seemed impressed. I heard the sink and my mom reacted too.

"What a sweet boy," she said and looked at my dad. He looked deep in thought, so I took the opportunity to carry my dishes in.

"So?" Noah asked as I helped him load the dishwasher.

"Things are looking good," I smiled. Noah grinned and finished with my plate and let me turn the dishwasher on.

"C'mon," I said and took his hand. My dad was back in the living room and I assumed my mom was in the bathroom.

"Noah, do you want to hang around or do you need to get

going?" my dad asked. Noah pulled out his phone for the first time of the night and I noticed several notifications as he quickly scrolled through them.

"Ah, I probably should get going. I have some homework to finish up," Noah said, and I felt slightly disappointed.

"Alright," my dad began and stood up. "Well kid, it was nice meeting ya," my dad said and held his hand out. Noah shook it firmly and smiled.

"Thank you for having me. Thank your wife for me as well, please," Noah said. My dad nodded, and Noah turned to me.

"I'll walk you out," I said and followed Noah out to his bike. He stopped and turned to look at me, "That went amazing," I said to him.

"Yeah, not nearly as bad as I had expected. Jackie's dad had his gun in the dining room," Noah laughed lightly.

"Ha… weird," I said. "Well, I'll see you tomorrow?" I added.

"Yep, and you're coming to the game?" he asked. I groaned teasingly and put my arms around his waist.

"If I have to."

Noah laughed and leaned down to peck my lips.

"I'm driving the Jeep tomorrow cause it's supposed to rain, so we could go to Rex's again? Our after-game tradition?" he asked.

"Sure," I said. He smiled and cupped my face in his palms kissing me gently.

"Get inside," Noah smirked when he pulled away.

"Mhm, drive safe, text me when you get home," I said.

"I will. Goodnight, Aria," he said.

"Night, Noah," I said and pecked his lips once again before walking back up to the house and watching him leave from the doorway.

Christina and I haven't talked about the kiss. And I didn't want to bring it up, so the topic hasn't come up, nor been discussed.

We walked through the gate of the stadium and stood along the sidelines as the teams got in position.

"About the party the other night," Christina began.

"Yeah?" I asked.

"Did I see you and Noah making out? Or was I drunk off my ass?" she asked. I watched as Noah tackled someone and the whistle blew.

"Both," I said, and she hit my arm.

"What! Oh my god!" she squealed.

"Shh!" I scolded.

"You two?!"

"Stop! You can't say anything!" I said.

"Yeah... Right... Totally," she said and looked out at the field. "This is amazing," she added. I laughed lightly as the snap of the ball grabbed my attention. Noah was looking where to throw the ball when a guy ran around and pummeled him to the ground.

"Oh!" was heard from the crowd. The player stood up and offered his hand to Noah, but my heart stopped. Another whistle sounded, and the coach ran out to the field.

"Noah!" I heard a feminine screech and Jackie dropped her pom poms running onto the field, shortly followed by Noah's dad. I started to move forward, and Christina grabbed my arm stopping me.

"Oh god," she said quietly, and I watched as the medics drove around the track and helped Noah up and into the ambulance. Jackie climbed in and Noah's dad rushed out of the stadium.

"Can you d-drive me to the hospital?" I asked my voice involuntarily quivering.

"Of course, c'mon," she said quickly and took my hand as we rushed out to her car.

Christina dropped me at the entrance and went to park her car. I walked in and went to approach the counter when I saw Noah's dad talking to a nurse outside a room. He walked with her and I approached the room and heard voices,

"Do you need anything?"

I peeked inside to see Jackie sitting on the edge of his bed.

"No," he answered. They shared a moment of silence until she spoke again.

"I miss you," she said.

"I miss you too," he said, and I noticed Christina. I moved away from the door and she walked over.

"She's still here?" Christina asked quietly.

"Yeah," I said, and she took a seat on a bench. I heard Jackie move so I turned my back and pretended to be signing a paper as she walked out. I looked at Christina and she nodded toward Noah's room. I walked in and he looked at me,

"Hey," he said.

"Are you okay?"

"Mild concussion," he said.

"I saw Jackie," I added.

"Yeah."

"You miss her?" I asked, my voice cracking. I cleared my throat and Noah looked away from me.

"Not her... necessarily. Just the way things were-."

"Before you met me?" I snapped. Noah looked at me and I could tell he regretted it.

"Hear what you wanna hear," he sighed and rolled his eyes. I glared at him and I heard footsteps enter the room.

"Visit's over," his dad said. I looked at Noah and he closed his eyes, so I made my way out.

The whole weekend passed, and I didn't hear from Noah. My subconscious was reminding me he was injured and was probably just resting, but Noah and Jackie's conversation replayed in the back of my mind.

I walked into the school and saw Noah with his back against his locker. He had a small bruise above his left eye and I smiled, but it faded quickly as Jackie came into view. She put her hand on his forehead and he actually smiled at her and laughed while pulling her hand away and holding it.

"What a dick."

I turned, and Christina stood next to me.

"Must've bumped the last few brain cells he had left loose," I commented as I walked off to class.

I sat at my desk and Noah strolled in with his books and looked right at me.

"Hey," he said as he sat down. Hey? He never said anything to me. I waited for a note to fall on my desk through the entire class, but instead I was dismissed by the bell. Noah stood and walked off to his next class and I collected my things, huffing to myself as I walked out of the room and bumped into someone who wasn't moving.

"Oh, sorry!" I said. The girl had hot pink nails, brown hair with a lot of blonde highlights, and a clear spray tan.

"It's fine. Um, do you know where room 8C is?" she asked me.

"Yeah, top floor," I responded.

"Thank you. I'm Madison," she said.

"Aria," I responded.

"I'll see you around!" she said and ran off.

I found Christina at lunch and she pulled me to sit next to her.

"I met Jackie's evil twin today," she said.

"Evil twin?" I asked.

"I mean, they don't look a lot alike but there's a new girl!" she continued.

"Madison?" I asked.

"Yeah! You met her already?" Christina asked.

"Earlier. You don't like her?" I asked.

"She's Noah's chemistry partner," Christina shared. Ooohh...

"It's just chemistry," I shrugged, and Christina rolled her eyes at me.

The rest of the day all I could think about was losing Noah. Instead of walking home, I stood outside the weight room and hid on the other side of the building and waited for Noah to walk out. They couldn't really make him do too much, so hopefully he was just hanging around. When he walked out, I threw a rock at him and he spun around to look. I waved him over to me and he looked around before rushing over and around the corner, out of sight from the field.

"Hey," I said pulling the sleeves of my shirt over my hands nervously. Noah nodded, and I looked around him.

"I don't want to lose you. And I'm sorry about Friday night but it pissed me off that I couldn't run and be by your side, but she could! And..." I trailed off and shook my head. Noah watched me carefully and nodded.

"Okay."

"That's it?" I asked.

"Aria... I really need a tutor..." Noah began and smirked. My smile spread across my face as he leaned down and pressed a tender kiss to my lips.

"You wanna come over then?" I asked.

"You can come over to my house. My dad is out of town," he said.

"Okay, I'll go wait," I said and made my way over to a bench outside the stadium and pulled out my Algebra II homework. I was right, Noah wasn't doing much physically for practice. He lifted weights for a little while but was looking over some of the play books until they let him leave a little early. He walked out and motioned for me to follow him to the Jeep.

I texted my mom and let her know I was tutoring Noah before we climbed out of the car and walked inside.

"What're you hungry for?" Noah asked.

"I thought you needed help?" I asked.

"Nope. Just wanted to have a simple date with my girlfriend," Noah laughed lightly.

"Oh," I said and walked into the living room. Noah joined me as we sat on the couch and I curled up to his side. "Why does your dad hate me?" I asked.

"He doesn't hate you," Noah said. I looked up at him, not believing a word he said. "I think he's just worried we're going to get serious. He was okay with Jackie... and such. But you're different," he said. I played with my hair and Noah pulled me close as we laid down and I closed my eyes.

"Dad, you're gonna wake her up," I heard Noah's voice.

"I don't give a shit. Why are you constantly disobeying me? Hm? I said Jackie, or no one. Football, or you move the fuck out!"

"Mom is probably rolling in her grave watching what a monster her husband has turned into," Noah spat.

"You're being an entitled piece of shit!" his dad yelled, and I sat up, intentionally making noise. They stayed silent and Noah came in.

"Hey, I let you sleep. I made dinner," Noah said.

"Okay, I'll be in," I said and watched him disappear. I was really getting sick of his dad managing to come home every time we had plans. I could make it through dinner with his dad. He made it through dinner with mine. I walked in the kitchen to see Noah had my plate set up next to him. They were both eating and from the entryway they looked the exact same. Their posture was formal, yet a slight curve of their back as they slouched a little.

"Good evening, Mr. Turner," I said kindly.

"Hi, Aria," he said. Noah looked at his dad and I was surprised he even remembered my name. I sat down and began eating what tasted like a chicken alfredo.

"This is really good, Noah," I said as I ate.

"It is," his dad agreed, and I turned to look at him.

"What do you do for work, Mr. Turner?" I asked. Noah's dad raised his eyebrows when he realized I was, in fact, talking to him.

"I'm a senior manager at Wolfstein Advertising. I work in marketing," he shared.

"Oh, sounds like a lot of hard work," I said.

"Four-year degree and ten years of dedication," he said. I took a sip of my water and his dad spoke up,

"My name is Robert, you can call me Rob," he said. I nodded, and Noah stood up to clean off his plate. I continued eating and Robert walked his plate over to the sink and loosened his tie. "Get her home at a decent time," his dad said before disappearing upstairs. Noah and I cleaned up and collapsed back on the couch afterward.

"I can't believe he was calm..." Noah said after we sat in silence for a few minutes.

"Who knows," I said, and Noah looked at the clock on the cable box beneath the table.

"You want me to take you home? It's a quarter 'til nine," he said.

"Yeah. I can't believe my parents haven't sent me anything," I said. I collected my things and followed Noah out to the Jeep.

Once he parked in the driveway I didn't want to get out. I looked at Noah and he grabbed my hand lightly.

"What?" he asked. I leaned across the console and kissed him. I felt his hands cup my face gently and I smiled at him when I pulled away. "Want me to walk you up?" he asked.

"No, then I'd want you to stay."

"You know I would."

"I know, but my parents wouldn't let you, so..." I said and opened the door.

"Night, Aria," he called and smiled at me as I looked back at him and shut the door.

November

Today was the day of the last football game. I already had it planned. I want to go to Rex's Diner afterward with Noah. Christina and I walked along the track around the field and occasionally stopped to watch a play here and there.

"I can't believe they're letting Noah play," she said.

"It's his last game. He wanted to," I said recalling the conversation we had the other night.

"I know, but really..." she said and stopped walking when she noticed Madison walking toward us.

"Aria!" Madison grinned at me.

"Hey, what's up?" I asked.

"Not a whole lot. What're you guys up to this weekend?" she asked.

"Mainly homework," Christina answered.

"Yeah, I'm not super loaded so I am spending time with my family," I added.

"Okay, well maybe I'll see you guys around!" she said and walked off.

"We should've invited her to go to the movies tomorrow," I frowned after she walked off.

"What? No! Absolutely not, that's our thing!" Christina scolded. I laughed and waited out the rest of the game for Noah.

"Want me to wait?" Christina asked as I stood by Noah's Jeep.

"No, he'll drive me home," I said. She nodded and walked to her car. Noah came out with his duffle bag and he looked confused.

"Aria?" he asked.

"Hey, wanna go to the diner?" I smiled. Noah frowned, and I shifted on my feet.

"I'm just going home. I am really tired," he said.

"Oh, okay."

"Is Christina still here. I could drop you off at home-?"

"She's not, but I'll call her-."

"Don't be ridiculous. I can drive you home," he said, and I nodded.

Noah parked in the driveway with a yawn before grabbing my hand.

"I'm sorry about tonight."

"Don't be. Go home and get some sleep," I said. He smiled and kissed the back of my hand before letting go and wishing me a goodnight.

I called Noah when I woke up the next morning and got sent to voicemail. I hung up and put my phone away, wanting to get ready to see the next Sherlock Holmes movie with Christina. Whenever there was a film with one of our favorite actors, we started going together. The fun part was always choosing candy beforehand.

"Two Sour Patch Kids," Christina said as I grabbed my drink and a box of the candy. Once she paid and we turned, I bumped into the guy waiting behind me.

"Oh, sorry," I said, and he smiled.

"No problem. Uh, I'm Ryker," he said to me. Christina walked away, and I grew nervous.

"Aria," I said.

"Nice to meet- well bump into- you," he smiled. His brown shaggy hair fell in his face as I nodded and turned to walk away. "Wait! Could I get your number?" he asked. I looked at him and Christina approached.

"No," I said, and he frowned.

"She means yes," Christina interrupted, and I eyed her.

"I said-."

"It's 555-8132," she said, and the guy frantically added it to his phone.

"I'll text you!" he called. I nodded and looked at Christina as we walked down the hall.

"Why'd you do that? I have a boyfriend!" I pointed out.

"Yes, but that doesn't mean you can't make other friends," she said.

After the movie, Christina and I walked out to her car.

"You want me to drop you off at Noah's?" she asked. I checked my phone and saw nothing from Noah.

"Yeah, I'm actually a little worried," I said.

"Okay," she responded, and I pointed her in the direction of Noah's house. His motorcycle was in the driveway, but the Jeep was gone. I motioned for her to wait as I rang the doorbell. I waited for a bit until I heard soft steps beyond the door.

"Aria, what're you doing here?" Robert asked.

"Hi, um, I was worried about Noah. Is he here?" I asked.

"No. He stopped home for about ten minutes last night and said he was meeting with a girl named Madison," he said.

"Madison?" I croaked.

"Yeah, is everything okay?" he asked.

"I guess I'll find out," I sighed. "Thanks," I added and walked back to Christina's car.

Noah's POV

"Mads, we've been in and out since eleven last night. It's almost one and I need to get home," I sighed as I closed my chemistry book.

"Are you sure?" She frowned. After I took Aria home last night, I ran home to change into some comfortable clothes and pull an all-nighter with Madison to finish this damn project. We still had a bit to do since we'd involuntarily begin to doze off.

"Yeah, my girlfr-," I stopped myself, but Madison caught on.

"Girlfriend? Who!" she smiled.

"It's no one..." I said and shook my head.

"Sounds like you're unhappy..."

"What? No, no, I'm happy," I said as I stood and collected my things.

"Then who is she?" Madison pressed.

"She goes to another school."

"That's why I haven't heard. Last I knew Jackie was the problem,"

"Problem?" I asked.

"She's in the way... I think we'd be cute," Madison smiled.

"Pardon?" I croaked.

"You know, at prom?" she asked.

"Oh, prom! Right! Yeah, that's... kinda far," I rambled as I grabbed my keys.

"Tell your girlfriend to keep you on a very-very tight leash," Madison smirked as I backed my way out of the house.

"Sure will, see you Monday!" I called and rushed out to my

car. Why was my face hot?

I walked inside the house and threw my bag down as I walked into the kitchen and started a pot of coffee. I'll just get myself around and go see Aria…

"Where were you?"

I turned, and my dad stood, leaned against the island.

"I told you I went to Madison's. Why do you care?" I asked pouring the coffee in the pot and hitting brew.

"I wasn't concerned until Aria stopped by," he said. My phone died while I was sleeping… shit.

"What'd you tell her?" I asked frantically.

"Exactly what I knew."

"She probably thinks I was cheating on her!" I yelled and pulled out my phone to plug it in.

"My question is why you wouldn't tell her where you were?" my dad pressed.

"I thought I'd be back by like eight and be able to get some sleep," I commented. "Did she look upset?" I asked and looked at him.

"Heartbroken," he answered and walked out.

Aria's POV

I pulled my phone away from my ear again to see if Noah was going to answer me.

"Don't you like popcorn?" I heard Ryker's voice making me return my phone to my ear.

"God, no! It gets stuck in your gums!" I complained, and Ryker laughed. We had been on the phone for the last hour and I found out he went to Emerson High, roughly twenty minutes away and was a senior like Noah. He was a gamer but enjoyed movies and playing soccer.

"I've enjoyed talking to you," Ryker said.

"Me too, it's been nice," I replied and rolled over to see Noah in my doorway. I jumped, and he watched me. "Uh, I gotta go," I said.

"Everything okay?" Ryker asked, and I knew Noah could hear his voice.

"Yeah, I'll talk to you later," I said and hung up. "You're okay?" I asked and sat up.

"Who was that?" he asked.

"A guy I met today, where were you?" I asked.

"Why are you changing the topic?" Noah asked.

"I-I'm not. I'd just like to know what was so important that you ignored me all day?" I asked.

"I had other plans. Are you cheating on me?" Noah spat. I shook my head and threw my hands up.

"Me? Me cheating on you? What about Madison? She was your other plans?" I asked growing irate.

"You know Madison. What about this guy, who is he?" Noah asked.

"What's it to you?"

"I'm your boyfriend, I'd like to know who he is…" Noah said. "Unless he's more important."

I sighed and shook my head, "You didn't tell me where you were last night and you're pulling the "I'm your boyfriend, I should know" shit?" I asked. Noah shook his head and backed away.

"No, I'm not pulling anything. It's none of my concern, you know why?" he asked, and I shook my head. "We're done," he said and spun around, walking out of the room, his feet pounding against the floor as he stormed out. I stood there and tried to process the entire argument. He just dumped me.

Wait...

He dumped me.

The tears came once my mind processed everything and I climbed back in my bed.

I missed school the next morning, my mom knew why; but she didn't tell my dad. The only thing on my mind was how Noah and I could've talked it out. I just wanted answers. My phone went off a quarter after three and I rolled over to see Christina was calling. It wasn't Noah, but I couldn't leave her without an explanation.

"Hey," I answered groggily from not using my voice all day.

"Hey? Where are you!" she exclaimed.

"Home."

"Why? Noah asked where you were too. Did something happen?"

"Yeah, I don't know why he cares. He dumped me."

"Wait, what?"

"Yeah," I said and curled back into my pillow.

"I'm so sorry, Aria. What the hell? He didn't say anything," she said.

"I wouldn't expect him to," I scoffed. I didn't think I'd be bitter about this, but the more time I had to think the worse it was.

"I'm coming over, we're going out," she said.

"A party at Matt's house. Wow, Noah totally won't be here!" I said, sarcasm laced in my voice.

"Someone else is here too," she said, and I looked around for a moment before she spun me in the right direction. Ryker stood next to a few guys who were into programming at school.

"Oh," I said quietly.

"Spend some time with Ryker. Let Noah see you don't need him! He couldn't show you off, but Ryker can!" Christina said and nudged me forward. I approached Ryker and tapped his shoulder.

"Aria! Hey, you never called me back!" Ryker said. His green eyes were full of concern as his brown locks fell into his face once again.

"Yeah, I'm sorry about that. Last night a lot went down," I said tucking some hair behind my ear.

"You wanna go out back and talk?" he asked. I shook my head and glanced up to see Noah talking to Jackie. When my eyes reached his they were cold. The warm and boldness in his eyes vanished to insecurity that only I could see. Ryker tapped my arm gently and handed me a cup.

"Who'd you show up with?" he asked as we began to step side to side along with the music.

"My friend, Christina, from the movies," I said.

"Oh, okay," he said, and I backed into someone.

"Sorry," I said when I noticed Madison.

"Hey, girl! I didn't know you'd be here! Who's this?" she asked.

"I'm Ryker."

They introduced themselves and shook hands before Madison laid eyes on Noah and Jackie.

"That liar," she commented. I looked over in confusion.

"Liar?" I asked.

"He said he had a girlfriend... and it wasn't Jackie," she huffed, and my guilt piled up. He wasn't cheating on me. I may have lost the best thing that had happened to me because I didn't think I was good enough. Madison walked off and Noah's eyes connected with mine again. I was hoping the apology in my eyes was clear.

"You know that guy?" Ryker asked, and I returned my attention to him.

"Yeah, we go to school together," I said, and Ryker watched me closely.

"That's not all…" he said, and I started to panic. "Let me take you home," Ryker said and walked me outside. He led me to a Honda Civic and opened the door for me.

After pointing Ryker to my home, we sat in the driveway.

"Are you okay?" he asked. That was all it took for my tear gates to flood.

"Noah and I have been dating since late September… and we got in a fight," I began as I explained the whole story to Ryker to the best of my ability.

"Oh," he said.

"I'm sorry."

"For what? I'm more than happy being friends," Ryker said as Noah pulled up on his motorcycle and climbed off. He came up to Ryker's window and knocked before motioning for him to roll the window down. Ryker pressed the button and Noah gave him a small smile before turning to me.

"Can we talk?"

I nodded, and Noah walked up to the front porch as I turned to Ryker.

"Thank you for the ride," I said.

"Not a problem. Let me know how everything goes," he smiled.

"I will. Thank you, bye," I said and hugged him before climbing out and joining Noah on the bench we had on our porch.

"Before we start… I'm way better looking than him," Noah said, and I rolled my eyes.

"Noah-."

"Right. Too soon," he said.

"What the hell?" I sighed.

"I made a mistake. Everything the last few weeks has been insane. Between Jackie, the team, my dad, school in general, and you…" he said and shook his head. I waited to see what else he had to say. "I didn't tell you about going over to Madison's because of how excited you were to go to the diner after the game. I figured we'd get the project done, I could run home and rest before taking you out for lunch… It was stupid," he sighed.

"I shouldn't have yelled at you about Ryker. You had a right to know who he was," I said, and Noah shook his head, grabbing my hands.

"None of this is your fault. It's entirely mine," Noah said, his brown eyes returned to the warm honey it had been before.

"Now what?" I asked. Noah smiled softly before looking across the yard.

"I'll see you at school?" he shrugged. What did that mean? I eyed him, and he pressed a sweet kiss to my lips.

"Oh, so we're… fine?" I asked, hope in my expression.

"Do you want to be fine? Cause I can get mad?" he asked, and I pushed him.

"No! We're great," I smiled. Noah stood up and tucked his hands in the pockets of his jeans.

"Night, Aria."

"Goodnight, Turner," I replied with a grin.

Thanksgiving

After talking to my parents, and much convincing, they allowed me to invite Noah over to have dinner with us. My grandparents from my father's side were lucky enough to join us. They arrived early in the morning and grandma stood in the kitchen talking about the most recent phone scam she had been receiving. When the doorbell rang, the entire house grew silent.

"Look at that motorbike!" my grandpa's voice echoed into the kitchen.

"Motorbike? Whose got one of those?" my grandma asked as I snuck out of the room and greeted Noah at the door.

"Hey," he smiled as he held a pan.

"Afternoon, what do you have?" I asked as he carried the pan into the kitchen.

"Dessert for later," he smiled and looked at my mom.

"May I put this in the fridge?" he asked.

"Go right ahead," she said.

"Grandma, this is Noah Turner, my boyfriend," I said.

"Oh, hello," she smiled at him.

"Hi, nice to meet you," Noah said, and I grabbed his hand.

"Is this another one of your mom's recipes?" I asked.

"It is. Strawberries and pretzels… almost like a cheesecake… you'll see," he said.

"You cook?" Grandma asked.

"Yeah, my mom taught me a bit before she passed,"

"That's very special," she said as I tugged lightly on his arm.

"Grandpa's watching football with dad," I said, and he followed as we entered the living room. There they sat watching the Chicago Bears once again. They get together at least once a year to watch the Bears.

"Ah, there he is! Dad, this is Aria's boyfriend, Noah Turner. School's quarterback," my dad said.

"Hello, nice to meet ya, son!" he said.

"Where's your dad, Noah?" my dad asked.

"He wanted to stay home," Noah said lightly, and my grandpa clapped.

"Good, more food!" he laughed, and Noah smiled as well. Noah and his dad stopped celebrating Thanksgiving once his mom grew sick. They both were out of thanks, now Noah just wanted to get back in the spirit.

"We're gonna help mom and grandma," I said.

Noah sat next to me at dinner and everything was going fantastic. Grandpa and Noah were picking on me- and my dad even chimed in. It was almost like Noah and I saw our future together that night. As we finished our food and faced one another the room fell silent. I was surrounded by people I loved, and my heart had never felt so full.

"Oh, wow! It's snowing!" my mom said from the kitchen.

"Is it sticking?" my grandpa asked.

"Yeah, the cement is starting to get covered," she said, and I looked at Noah and he froze.

"Let's get your bike in the garage," my dad said and they both excused themselves as I helped my mom clear the table. When they came back in, my dad looked at my mom.

"Looks like he's staying tonight. The driveway was slick, on that bike he'll barely make it down the street," my dad said, and I couldn't help the smile that spread upon my face. "On the couch!" he added as he walked into the living room. Noah made himself useful and started to put extra dishes away, but I noticed the smirk across his face as well.

It didn't take long to clean the table with more of us and not long after my grandma came in with a board game.

"Let's play Scrabble!" she said. My grandpa pointed to Noah and grinned.

"Let's go pretty boy!" Grandpa challenged. I laughed and joined the table as my mom went into the living room and my dad came in with his coat on.

"I'm gonna shovel," he announced.

We got the game set up and I looked at my seven letters, D D I O A T. Okay… I looked at the board and looked at what my grandparents placed. Quickly and Riding. Noah was pondering so I put down T and O off the G to create Tog.

"Oh, come on, Aria!" my grandma said. I shrugged shyly as Noah placed down "U L I P" off my T. My grandma added BOW to the L in quickly to create Blow, only for my grandpa to add Job onto it. Noah and my grandpa high-fived leaving me blushing crimson.

"Okay, Aria," my grandma cheered. I laughed and looked at my selection, "D I P E N K C". I added, "DCK" to my I in Tulip to make Dick. My grandma laughed, and I couldn't bring myself to look at Noah as laughter erupted around the table.

After we finished the game, my grandparents made their way to the guest room as I brought down a pillow and blanket for Noah.

"Here," I said and handed them to him.

"Thanks, I texted my dad and let him know."

"Is he okay with it?"

"Yeah, he didn't mind at all," he shrugged.

"Okay," I said and started to lay out the blanket for him when he stopped me.

"I got it," he said smiling at me.

"Okay, goodnight."

"Goodnight," he said quietly and pecked my lips.

December

It was the time of year again where we had two weeks of school before being free for the rest of the year. It was also the time of extreme stress for almost every student, Noah being one of them. He had been applying to colleges and trying to study for exams. I tried to help, but I didn't know the material well enough, so Noah had to start getting tutored from a senior instead.

The football team was holding a bake sale to raise money for the team. This was time for Noah and I to spend together. We made apple cinnamon brownies and we took some time to package them with cute bows too.

"These are great," Noah said as we stood in his kitchen.

"Yeah, I can't wait to see if your dad likes them," I said as Noah's phone went off on the counter.

"Hey?" he answered. I started cleaning as Noah finished one of the brownies he was eating. "Don't worry, we can double up tomorrow night," Noah said, and my stomach fluttered. It sounded like his tutor was canceling his session. I began to get excited as Noah hung up and turned to me.

"Who was that?" I asked.

"Paul, my tutor, said he had a family emergency."

"Oh, so you're staying home?" I asked.

"Yeah."

"Yes! Oh my gosh! Let's decorate! Put up a Christmas tree-!"

"Woah, Aria... We haven't done that the last two years..." Noah said.

"Let's do it. Maybe your dad will appreciate it?" I tried. Noah thought for a moment before shrugging.

"I'll bring the tree up from the basement," he said. I finished cleaning the kitchen as Noah brought up the tree and a few boxes.

"What's in the boxes?" I asked.

"Ornaments, lights..." he shrugged. I nodded as we cleared a spot in the corner of the living room. He put up the tree and we turned on some Christmas music as we wrapped the tree in lights and started decorating. The slam of the front door caught our attention as Robert walked in.

"Hey, dad!" Noah said.

"Hi... What's all this?" Robert asked.

"Just getting in the spirit. We made brownies too!" I smiled.

"Don't you have a study session?" his dad asked.

"I was supposed to. Paul canceled so we decided to decorate," Noah said. His dad looked at the tree and I motioned to the kitchen.

"We left you a brownie," I added. Robert walked over, and I joined him as Noah continued to decorate the tree. He sat at the island and took a bite before his eyes lit up.

"Oh, wow!" he said.

"I found the recipe online," I shrugged.

"It's still really good," he complimented.

"Thank you."

Robert's eyes wandered over to Noah who was wrapping garland around the tree.

"Noah?" Robert called.

"Yeah?" Noah asked as he came into the kitchen with us.

"The living room looks great," he said.

"Really?" Noah smiled.

"Yeah, and since both of you are here... There's something I'd like to tell you," Robert began. I felt confusion spread across my face, as it did on Noah's.

"Is everything okay?"

"Yeah, yes. Great actually, I met someone," he said. *Oh no.* I looked at Noah and he stared at his father.

"Y-You what?"

"I met someone. Her name is Chantel, she works with me," Robert said. Noah's eyes didn't leave his father as he spoke.

"And you just decided to move on?" Noah spat. I could see the anger boiling inside him, the vein in his neck popping out.

"Noah, you don't understand. Your mom-."

"My mom deserved so much better than you!" Noah yelled and stormed off upstairs. His dad sat there and we both took in the silence.

"His mother and I discussed this. We decided I need to live my life too," he sighed.

"I get it, she wanted you to be happy," I said.

"Exactly," Robert said.

"I'll talk to Noah, I promise," I said.

"Thank you."

"No thanks needed. Where's his room?" I asked.

"You haven't been up there?" he asked.

"No..."

"Up the stairs, second door to the right," he said. I walked upstairs and opened the door to see Noah seated on the edge of his bed, his head down.

"Noah, are you okay?" I asked. He didn't speak as I shut the door and walked over to sit with him. I heard him sniff and a small hiccup. I put my arms around him and his face fell into my chest.

Two and a half months ago I would have never imagined seeing Noah bawl his eyes out. It was strange, but I felt for him. Noah sat up a few minutes later and got himself to calm down.

"I... that was humiliating," Noah laughed at himself and shook his head.

"It's fine. Your dad had more to say," I said. Noah looked at me, so I continued. "He said they talked about it. Your mom wanted him to be happy and live his life," I shared. Noah nodded, and his eyes wandered to his end table. I looked and saw a photo of him and who I assumed was his mother in her hospital bed.

"Is that her?" I asked. He nodded, and I looked again. She was beautiful with long flowing red hair and pouty lips. Even in the situation she had a huge smile across her face. I looked around Noah's room and noticed he had some clothes tossed on the floor and his laptop was open on his desk with a few notebooks scattered around, his camera on top.

"I should probably drive you home," he said I shook my head and curled up with him.

"I'll stay over tonight. I'll just text my mom and say your dad is here," I said.

"Is that good enough?"

"We'll see," I shrugged. After texting my mom, she responded with an okay.

"She's okay with it. Let's go make dinner?" I asked. He nodded and followed me downstairs.

Noah's POV

My phone went off with a message from someone on Instagram. They were following nearly two thousand accounts and had twenty followers. The bio read, "Get to know me" with a winky face. I clicked on the message to read,

"Hi Noah!"

I furrowed my eyebrows and responded.

"Uh, hi... who is this?"

They answered right away.

"Just call me Nonnie!"

"As in... anonymous?" I sent back.

"Ohhhh! You're smart!" a message snapped back. I backed out of the messages and looked at their only post. It was a screenshot from their notes on their phone.

"About GoSaintsGo:

Likes:

-Water

-Men. Preferably Tall.

-Football/ Basketball/ Baseball

-Reading

-Cuddling

-Hiking

-Cooking

-Dogs

Am a hopeless romantic. Just want to curl up I your arms, watch a movie, and feed you popcorn.

Dislikes:

-Liars

Message me if curious."

Interesting.

"I just read your profile." I messaged back.

"What do you think?"

"Noah?" Aria asked.

"Yeah?"

"You gonna help?" she asked.

"Yeah, sorry. Matt was asking if we made anything for the bake sale," I lied and sent back,

"We have a lot in common... but I'd like to know who you are."

We made dinner and ate as I swiped my phone and ran off to the bathroom to see Nonnie responded.

"I'd like to get to know each other a little more."

I rose my eyebrows and replied,

"What makes you think I'll share anything?"

"You're curious," was sent back.

"Can you at least send me a photo so I know what you look like?" The bubble came up and a response appeared.

"A photo? That's a lot to ask for so soon..."

"I'll send one," I sent back.

"Please do. I can scroll through your profile though."

I quickly exited the app and went through my phone when I found one from last winter.

"Here's one I haven't posted." I typed and sent it along with a photo of myself.

"Very very cute."

"Now you," I sent.

A selfie came in of a beautiful girl with brown hair and blonde highlights, her smile wide.

I hit the heart and it sent as she replied with a winky face.

"You're beautiful," I sent.

"Thank you, you are pretty hot," she responded. I sent a gif of Obama saying Thank You, and another message came in.

"I'll ttyl."

My concern started to turn into confusion.

"Um ok?" I sent back.

Aria's POV

When I entered the school the next morning, Christina put her arm locked around mine.

"You are gonna want to see this..." she said and handed me her phone. It was screenshots of an account by the name of 'go-saintsgo' messaging Noah.

"He said she's beautiful. I reverse looked up the photo of the girl, it's a stock photo," Christina said.

"He was gonna cheat on me..." I mumbled.

"Hm?"

"Nothing... who leaked this?"

Christina went to reply as Noah opened his locker and tons of papers with the screenshots fell out. I picked one up that slid across the floor and the word CHEATER written across the page in red sharpie. Jackie looked at one of them and started laughing.

"Who are you cheating on?" Jackie laughed.

"Wait, what?" Madison asked and pushed me aside. Noah's eyes fell on me and I looked away.

"What?" Jackie asked Madison.

"You're not together?" Madison asked.

"No! We broke up a while ago."

"I-I- you said you had a girlfriend!" Madison snapped at Noah. My head was spinning as I watched the principal stomp down the hall and take Jackie, Madison, and Noah to his office.

My phone went off in my first class with messages from Noah that I didn't check until lunch.

"Are you okay?"

"You knew I wasn't cheating."

"I would never cheat on you."

"I am so sorry."

"Please call me later."

"Don't leave me like this. At least let me explain."

I put my phone down and Christina joined me at the table.

"Maybe you should go public?" she asked as soon as she sat down.

"Why? We're over," I shrugged. This was the second time in only two weeks.

"Why? Madison was screwing with him!"

"Still! He kept messaging her! If I let this slide, he'll do it again. Whoever gets him next can thank me," I said.

"No," Christina said.

"Excuse me?"

"No! You two really like each other! No, you LOVE each other. And I know it!"

"I don't love him," I argued.

"Yes! You do! You totally do!"

"Christina, enough," I glared and stood up.

"Aria!" Madison smiled and approached me with her tray. Without thinking, I hit it and it dumped all over her. Everyone grew quiet and my eyes landed on Jackie who smirked. I was just like her. I grabbed my water bottle and ran out of the cafeteria.

The end of the day could not come quick enough. I walked home, and a white 2016 Hyundai Elantra slowed beside me. The window rolled down and Jackie smiled at me.

"Aria need a ride?" she asked.

"Nope, I'm good," I responded.

"Let me rephrase that. We need to talk," she said, and I stopped.

"Why?"

"I appreciate what you did today. I saw it as you are sticking up for me," she said. Was she delusional?

"Okay."

"I was thinking we could go to the mall?" she asked.

"Ah, I would but I have homework..." I tried.

"Oh, shoot! Me too! You're an English tutor, right? I could use some help on my final paper," she said, and I sighed.

"Sure," I responded and climbed in the car with her, directing her to my house.

We entered the dining room and Jackie got set up when there was a knock on the front door. I walked over and opened it to see Noah.

"Hey, we need to talk," he said, and my eyes nearly popped out of my head.

"Noah?" I heard Jackie ask. His eyes widened as she joined me at the door. "What're you doing here?"

"Aria is my tutor," Noah said.

"Well, she's tutoring me tonight. I'm sure Madison would love to help you," Jackie remarked. Noah glared at her and pointed.

"Fuck you," he growled.

"As if you haven't already," She smirked. Noah's eyes fell on me and I looked at the ground.

"We'll reschedule," I lied and shut the door.

"What a lowlife," she spat and returned to the dining room.

Jackie left before dinner and my mom looked at me.

"She's interesting."

"Comes with the job," I lied.

"Still nice of you to tutor," she replied. The doorbell and my dad stood up in the living room.

"I got it," he said. I resumed helping my mom when someone cleared their throat.

"Robert?" I asked.

"Hello, Aria. May we go for a walk?" he asked. I nodded and walked with him outside.

"What're you doing here?" I asked.

"The principal called me in today. I heard everything... saw the messages," he said.

"And it was wrong," I stated.

"It was. I'm not disagreeing with you. But I know my son. He doesn't mope over a girl. Well, he hasn't until now," he said.

"Robert, I know what you're doing," I sighed.

"I'm telling you what is going on. I love my son, I do. I've hurt him, I've been awful to him, the least I can do is bring back one person he loves, and sadly his mother isn't an option. But you are," he said. I stood there and looked at him.

"I'll try to talk to him tomorrow," I said.

"He'll be at the recreation center meeting with the community winter football league," he said.

"Okay."

"Thank you, Aria."

"I didn't say I'm taking him back," I eyed Robert only to see a smirk across his lips.

"Oh-Kay," he answered as we stopped outside my driveway.

Christina parked outside the recreation center and looked at me.

"Want me to wait?" she asked.

"No."

"So, you're taking him back?" she smiled.

"We'll see... we just need to talk," I sighed.

"Okay, good luck," she said. I climbed out and got a text from Ryker asking if I wanted to hang out. I didn't respond as I walked inside and read the sign before me.

Swim- East Side

Basketball- North Gym

Football- North East Gym

I walked in and peeked inside to see several guys lines up in t-shirts and shorts. Noah held the ball and I slid inside and took a seat with some others who were watching. There was a cheer squad and one of the girls was watching Noah. I sat back through most of practice and Noah didn't notice me until half-way through. He waved, and I just nodded and looked away. I was still mad and hurt, but we had to talk this out.

They were dismissed by 6:45 and Noah approached the bleachers before getting stopped by the cheerleader who was asking him something. He shook his head no and backed away, so he could approach me.

"Hey," he said.

"Hi... I think we need to talk," I said and caught the girl watching me. "Who's that?" I asked. Noah sighed, and I noticed the whole squad looked too.

"That's Francesca," Noah answered.

"The chick you knocked up?" I asked. Noah cringed and put his hands out.

"Yeah... Can we talk about us now?"

"Okay... You cheated on me."

"I didn't mean any of it..."

"And you want me to believe that?"

"Yes. Aria, not telling anyone about us is extremely difficult," he said.

"I get that. But now it's either me, or your reputation because this is getting to be too much."

"Aria, it's only six more months..." Noah sighed.

"You're ridiculous," I glared.

"You want Jackie to know? Madison? You saw what happened... that could come between us. I really don't want that to happen to you. Please Aria... we can make this work. I miss you."

I stared at him and rolled my eyes.

"You're an idiot."

"I know," he said. I nodded, and Noah smiled. "Let me grab my things and I'll take you home," he said.

Christina had a doctor's appointment the next day, so I sat at lunch alone texting Ryker. We were in the middle of discussing if Batman or Superman was better when I felt someone sit with me.

"Aria Boyd," Jackie said.

"Yes?" I asked and sat my phone down. She slid her phone across the table to me and it was a photo of me and Noah at practice last night. My eyes widened and Jackie wasn't smiling. "That's not how it looks."

"Oh, yes, it is. He showed up at your house, he looked at you in the hall, I'm not stupid," Jackie stated.

"I don't want-."

"I'm not mad," she said.

"Hm?" I asked.

"And I won't say anything..."

"Why?"

"You're not Madison. I hate that bitch. I also am dating someone else, but I figured I'd let you know I told Fran to delete it."

"Fran?"

"Francesca? Yeah, we got close after Noah's mistake... I assume you know?"

"Yeah, I know."

"I'll keep an eye out. I'm sorry about everything before. You're really sweet," she said.

"Uh... thanks," I said as she stood and walked away. I still don't trust her. Every part of me wanted to panic, but at this point... I'd be okay with people knowing.

Noah picked me up a street away from the school and brought me back to his house.

"Just warning you, Chantel has been staying with us," he said.

"Okay," I shrugged.

"And dad mentioned having Christmas with her and you on the 23rd, then I can spend Christmas at your house?"

"Awesome, I like that idea."

We climbed out of the car and walked inside, making our way to the living room and plopping down on the couch. I leaned into Noah's side as he reached for the remote and began channel surfing.

"Anything look good?" he asked, and I stared at the side of

his face. My silence caught his attention as he looked down at me and I pressed my lips to his.

"You don't look too bad," I lightly flirted as he grinned and cupped my face with his hand while leaning in to kiss me again.

"Oh! Sorry-sorry!" we heard.

I pulled back and looked at a woman with black hair and heavily black eye lined green eyes.

"Chantel," Noah began, and she nodded.

"Right, right. Have fun you two! I won't tell your dad," she said and left the room.

"I don't like her," Noah muttered and put his elbows on his knees. I totally agreed with him but wanted to see him get closer with his dad. Maybe it won't last long? Or she'll get bored?

"Don't judge her too soon," I smiled lightly.

"You don't like her either," he said.

"I didn't say that. Give her a chance!"

Christmas

The Turner's

I spent hours trying to figure out what the best gift for Noah would be. A camera would be great, but I'm not rich. Even something for his motorcycle… but I had no clue. Knowing Noah even if I found something from the heart, it'd be just enough. As I walked through the strip mall, I found a bracelet, I didn't want to get him something so… girlie to wreck his hard exterior but what was on it changed my mind.

As I sat with Noah in the living room, his grandparents began to show up. I made sure I looked ten times more presentable than I usually do. I curled my hair, put on light makeup, wore a white button up and black dress pants. Robert was very impressed and thanked me for the effort made.

"You're the young lady Robert told me all about! Aria, correct?" Noah's grandma asked.

"Yes, nice to meet you," I said as I expected to shake her hand, but instead she hugged me.

"My name is Edna, this is my husband Edward."

"Nice to meet you both," I said.

"You go to school together?" his grandpa asked. Noah returned to my side and surprised me when he spoke.

"Yeah. Aria is a year younger than me. I bumped into her on the first day of school and then she ended up being my tutor."

"Isn't that cute?" Edna smiled and looked up at her husband.

"How was your football season?" Edward asked, and I used that opportunity to excuse myself from their conversation and enter the kitchen. I was going to ask Robert if he needed help with dinner, but I found Chantel instead. I hid in the hall and listened, realizing she was on the phone.

"Yeah, well his parents are over. Along with his son's girlfriend," she began. I felt a little guilty for eavesdropping, but I didn't want her to hurt Robert either.

"Look, I just have to wait till Robert is at work and Noah's girlfriend isn't around. He's got to be into older women, c'mon! A body like his-." I blocked the rest out as I returned to the living room. I approached Noah and he reached out for my hand, so I could join him on the couch.

"Can I talk to you alone for a moment?" I asked.

"Of course, excuse us," Noah smiled at his grandparents. He went to lead us to the kitchen, but instead I pulled him onto the back patio and shut the door.

"It's a little cold, are you alright?" he asked.

"Yeah. Uh, no... no not at all. I went into the kitchen to ask your dad if I could help with dinner and I heard Chantel on the phone-."

"Oh no."

"It's probably not what you think."

"She's cheating on my dad!"

"Not exactly. She likes you... or at least she's targeting you. She likes your body or whatever," I shivered, surprisingly not because of the cold. Noah didn't budge and not a muscle moved for nearly a minute. "Noah?"

"What the fuck?!" he finally spoke. I shrugged, and he looked at the door.

"What should we do?"

"We can pull your dad aside?" I tried.

"He already knows I hate her, he won't listen to me."

"Okay, I can tell him. After your grandparents leave."

"Can you do that?"

"Yes. You're my boyfriend, she isn't getting near you."

"You're kinda cute when you're protective," he smirked.

"Better get used to it," I smiled. Noah pecked my lips and put his forehead to mine. "Let's get back inside," I said, and we rejoined everyone in the living room.

"The tree looks great, Rob," Edna spoke.

"Thanks mom, that was all those two. We haven't put a tree up..." Robert paused and looked at Chantel. "For a while," he finished. Noah sat with me on the loveseat and put his arm around me.

"That's really sweet. I'm glad to see you both a lot happier," she said.

"Let me check on the food," Robert said, and I jumped up.

"I'll help," I said. I really needed to tell him now, or it would bother me all night. I followed him into the kitchen and he eyed me pointedly.

"Is something wrong?" he asked. I bit my lip in frustration. Why is this so difficult? My silence gained his full attention as he shut the oven and leaned forward against the island between us.

"Robert, Chantel isn't a good person," I began trying to tread carefully. He stood up straight and put his hands in his pockets.

"How so?"

"I overhead her on the phone. She was sexualizing Noah," I said. Robert looked at me long and hard. I was hoping he could see the worry and concern I had for Noah. "I'm only saying this because I care about my boyfriend and I don't want either of you getting hurt," I said. Robert nodded and rubbed his face much like Noah does when he's stressed or agitated.

"Okay. Go back in the living room," he said.

"I'm sorry, Robert," I said and walked around the counter to hug him.

I returned to the living room and Edna was passing around gifts. I was surprised when she handed me an envelope. Robert returned, we all opened everything, and I smiled at the gift card for the local café.

"Noah said you like coffee, I hope that's alright," she said.

"Yes! Very! Thank you so much, you didn't have to!" I said and heard the wrapping paper of my gift and faced Noah. He opened the box and revealed the silver bracelet with a polaroid photo engraved in it. He smiled and clipped it around his wrist. It wasn't flashy, so it didn't look quite as girlie as I thought.

"Thank you," Noah said and kissed me. Noah had a last gift from Chantel and I was nearly at the edge of my seat as he opened it to reveal a box of condoms. If Robert didn't believe me before, he should now. Edna looked at Chantel, as did I.

"Caught these two on the couch the other day, figured you'd need those," she said. Immediately Edna stood from the couch.

"Nothing happened on the couch, we kissed," I assured his grandmother.

"I thought they were going to swallow each other," she said. I felt a glare form on my face and Robert stepped in.

"Let's talk," he said and pulled her out of the room.

"That woman..." Edna said full of disgust.

"I know," I agreed. Noah sat the condoms down and stood up.

"I'll be right back," he said and entered the kitchen.

"Well... How'd you two meet?" I asked Edna. She smiled and sat back down beside her husband.

"We met in high school. He played basketball and I went to all the games wit my friends. After a while, I noticed he would look at me," she began.

"After one of the games she had approached me and asked if I had a problem," Edward added, and I laughed.

"We started dating the next day. He asked me out to dinner," she said. That was pretty close to Noah and me. I smiled at the floor when I heard the front door slam shut as Noah came in from the kitchen.

"Ah... dinner's ready," he announced. Robert walked in alone and we all moved to the dining room. Noah got all the food around and served all of us the ham Robert had prepared.

Dinner was silent as we ate. Robert looked upset and I felt guilty. I should have waited. Then the condoms would have seemed funnier. After eating, Noah's grandparents wanted to head home. We said our goodbyes and as soon as they left Robert disappeared upstairs.

"Let's clean up," I said as Noah opened the dishwasher.

Christmas Day

"Noah's here!" my dad announced as we raced to the door. He only won because he was in the living room. "Noah!" my dad greeted.

"Hi Sir."

"It's Edgar, son! Come in!" my dad said and led him into the living room to set down the gifts he brought.

"I said you didn't have to get anything!" I sighed as Noah approached me.

"I had to get something. I apologize, I'm not the best at picking gifts," Noah added looking at my parents.

"I'm sure you did just fine," my mom said. Noah smiled and looked at me. It almost seemed like he was nervous.

"Are you alright?" I asked quietly as my mom snuck off to the kitchen and my dad went to the bathroom before my grandparents showed up.

"Yeah, just a little nervous today," he shrugged.

"Don't be. My family loves you," I said.

"Good," he smiled and held my hand. As soon as my maternal grandmother showed up, she noticed Noah. I had called her several times and told her about him. We were really close. She gave him a hug and he held her tight.

"I've heard a lot about you," she said.

"Oh, man," Noah responded, and we laughed. My paternal grandparents came in later and remembered Noah, giving him hugs as well.

"Let's get to the presents!" my grandpa said, and he sat on the couch next to the tree.

"What'd you get me?" I asked Noah. His face turned pale as he took a slow breath in.

"It's not under the tree," he said.

We got down to Noah's gifts which he got my grandparents gift cards for the only nice restaurant in town, which was so expensive, the cheapest gift card started at one hundred dollars.

"Wow, thank you," my grandpa said, and my grandma was shocked as well. My dad tore into his that had both of my parents' names on it. Inside the box were two Chicago Bears winter hats, and two Trubisky jerseys.

"Oh wow!" my mom said when my dad jumped up out of his chair holding two tickets.

"Kid are you serious?" my dad asked. Noah smiled and nodded.

"Yeah, I know how much you love football. Figured you'd wanna go,"

"Thank you, Noah!" my mom smiled.

"And for you," Noah said spinning to face me. He stood up and took my hands to help me stand as well.

"The last four months with you have been some of the best I've ever had. After losing mom... I didn't know what to do, I admit I was lost and scared to even step foot in my own home. I want to make a promise to you, Aria," Noah reached into the pocket of his leather jacket and pulled out a small box. I started to panic. What is happening?

"Noah-."

"Aria, I promise every part of myself to you. Only you. My heart, my soul, my being is only for you... One day, we can be much more but for now... Can you promise yourself to me too?" Noah asked opening the box to a silver band with a heart and sapphire gem in the middle. My vision was blurry with tears as Noah stood in front of everyone I love most.

"Noah," I cried and pulled him into a hug. "Of course," I added, and he held me tight as my family clapped behind us.

"Oh, hold still! I need to take a photo!" my mom said and pulled out her phone. She pushed us over by the tree and we stood together as she snapped the photo.

January

Noah and I didn't get to spend New Year's together. The weather was rough, so we got on FaceTime and ended up blowing a kiss to each other and falling asleep. But now we were back at school, back to hiding our relationship.

"How was break?" Christina asked.

"Good. Um, Noah gave me this," I said and showed her the ring on my left hand.

"Oh my gosh! It's so cute!"

"I know, my family loves him. I just wish we didn't have to hide here."

"Only five more months. You're halfway there."

Noah walked in and opened his locker.

"Morning, ladies."

"Morning, Noah," Christina answered as she looked at me. "Ryker has a basketball game tonight, wanna go?" she asked.

"Okay, sure," I said when Noah cleared his throat and shook his head, no. I looked at Christina in confusion and shrugged. "I'll text you," I concluded. I walked past her to class and Noah followed close behind as we took our seats and he spun to look at me.

"I have practice tonight. Don't you wanna go?" he asked quietly. Nobody else wanted to go to class ten minutes early, so we were alone for now.

"Yes, but I should go support Ryker. I haven't seen him in a while, or spent time with Christina," I pointed out. Noah's eyes ran over my face before frowning.

"Okay, whatever," he shrugged.

"It's against our school, you could come after?"

"Maybe."

A classmate came in and Noah turned back around in his seat.

Noah's POV

No part of me wanted to go to this basketball game tonight. A few guys on the community team go to school with Ryker and speak very highly of him, but I still didn't like him.

"Is Ryker engaged?" I heard one of the guys ask next to me.

"I don't think so, why?" another guy asked. I walked over to see Ryker posted a photo of him hugging Aria, the ring I gave her in clear sight.

"No, that girl has a boyfriend. She goes to my school," I interjected.

"He could do way better. She's a little chunky."

"Seriously?" I spat and collected my things. As I climbed in my Jeep, I called Aria. I waited… and waited, not receiving an answer. I hung up and texted her.

"Everything okay?"

I drove home and checked my phone as I walked in the door. No response.

"Noah?"

I looked up from my phone to see my dad seated at the island, the mail in front of him.

"Two colleges sent something," he said. I walked over and saw one from UCLA… and Ohio State? I didn't apply to Ohio State.

"Ohio?" I asked.

"They're one of the best football schools. I sent one in for you," he said.

"Oh," I said and opened UCLA first. I was accepted for Photojournalism. I kept calm as I opened Ohio State next... I was accepted.

"Well?" my dad asked.

"T-They accepted me," I said.

"Awesome, let me see!" he said, and I handed him the paper, clenching my jaw. "What's wrong?" my dad asked.

"Nothing, I'd just like to think about it a little more before we make a decision."

"Noah, this is an amazing opportunity."

"I get that, but I'd like to think about it."

"I told you, the only way I'm paying for college is if your ass is on a field chasing a football. You understand me?" my dad glared and took the acceptance letter with him. I took the one from UCLA and went to my room.

Aria's POV

"I'm glad we got to hang out!" I smiled at Ryker and Christina as we left the café. After the game, we decided to catch up and grab some food. As we parted and I climbed in Christina's car, I checked my phone to see Noah tried to call me and he even texted and asked if everything was okay. I hit call back as Christina began driving me home.

"Hey," Noah answered sounding extremely upset.

"Are you okay?" I asked.

"Hm? Me? I'm fine. Just tired, how was the game?"

"They won, our team fought though."

"Are you home yet?"

"No, heading home now."

"Who's driving?"

"Christina, why?" I asked.

"Hi, Noah!" Christina called.

"Just wondering. You should come over after school tomorrow," he said.

"Okay..." We shared an awkward silence that I had to break. "Are you sure you're okay?"

"Yeah. Text me when you're home. I gotta go," he said and hung up. I put my phone down and frowned.

"Everything okay?" Christina asked.

"Noah sounded upset."

"Hmm, maybe he's PMS-ing," she shrugged.

As I walked to school the next morning, my question was answered as a text from Jackie came in.

"There's a rumor going around that you're pregnant, is it true?"

My eyes widened as I typed back.

"No! What rumor?"

Another text came in from Christina.

"People think Ryker knocked you up and that you're engaged after last night."

I felt my heart beating faster and faster. Oh no. Noah doesn't actually believe all this... Does he? I went to call Noah when a message from Jackie came in again. Okay, I'll just put my phone away and focus on finding Noah. I got into the school and stopped at my locker to put my things away before going straight to class, where Noah wasn't. I pulled my phone back out and texted him to ask if he was still taking me home after school. Maybe he was just coming in late? I didn't get a response until the end of the day.

"College visit this week. We'll talk Sunday when I get home."

We'll talk? I was nervous. What did he mean? Where was he visiting? That made me realize... he is graduating soon. We really did need to talk.

February

Noah came home today. I was typing up a paper when a FaceTime call came up on my laptop.

"Hey," he said once I answered.

"Hey, where are you?"

"About ten minutes outside town. We're gonna stop at home first so I can run my things inside."

"Okay."

"See ya in a few?"

"Yeah, bye."

"Bye."

I clicked out of FaceTime and decided to get up and stretch.

"Aria! Ryker is here!" my mom called up the stairs.

"Coming!" I called back and ran downstairs to meet Ryker on the porch.

"Hey, I heard about the rumors," he said.

"I know. I took down the photo of us and sent out a message saying we're good friends. I haven't said anything about Noah."

"Thank you."

"Of course, I didn't think it would lead to that."

"Me either, it was ridiculous."

"I heard guys at your school were making some nasty comments."

"Yeah, just things like 'she's not pregnant, just fat' and whatever," I shrugged.

"That's awful. How are you staying strong?"

"I have my family, friends, and an amazing boyfriend. What more could I want?" I asked.

"That's a great outlook, Aria Boyd."

"Thank you," I smiled and hugged him.

"Aria!"

I pulled away from Ryker to see Noah approaching.

"Noah, you're back!" I smiled, and he walked right past me and squared up to Ryker.

"Woah take it easy, Noah. Nothing is going on."

"What? Noah, you don't really think I'd cheat on you?" I asked him. He turned to look at me and I rose my eyebrows.

"I'm gonna go," Ryker said and patted my back before leaving.

"Noah?" I asked.

"It's not about Ryker..." he said. I watched as he looked around the yard and almost looked like he was going to cry. "My dad..."

"Is he hurting you again? Noah, I want you to talk to me."

"I'm trying!" he sighed. I stayed quiet as he calmed down. "He's just pushing me, and I don't know what I want yet..."

"With school?"

"With us."

"Oh?" I asked, and Noah took my hands.

"I didn't call or text you to see what would happen if we were apart. I knew you weren't like the others. Hell, I didn't even know what kind of ring to get you, I had to ask the sales associate," he laughed. "I kept thinking about you, over and over and over... I felt insane. I wasn't using my phone except to stalk you on social media and stare at you like a damn creep-."

"Noah."

"What?"

"It's okay," I laughed.

"It's not. Aria Jade Boyd, I love you."

The words that left his mouth had the most meaning I have ever head. The look of sincerity across his beautiful hazel eyes and the brown messy hair of his falling into his face. I was in love. I was deeply, madly in love with Noah Turner.

"I love you too," I said. Noah smiled at me and pulled me into his arms, pressing a kiss to my lips.

Valentine's Day

Noah's dad was out of town on work, so we had the house to ourselves. What I didn't expect was to walk into the house and see flowers on the island, along with a box of chocolate.

"Noah, I said not to get me anything!"

"Oh, well I guess you're going to be disappointed because there's several other gifts tonight, gorgeous," he said and kissed me. When we pulled apart his hand held up a necklace.

September.

"September?" I asked.

"When we started seeing each other... and 2018 on the back," he said. I smiled and kissed him again.

"You're spoiling me."

"Okay, you choose. Dinner or next surprise?" he asked.

"I think I'm up for another surprise," I smirked. Noah laughed at my response and took my hand, leading me upstairs. We walked into his room and I laughed.

"What?" he asked.

"This *is* a surprise... you cleaned your room," I giggled.

"Really?!" he laughed and pulled me to him as we fell back on the bed. Noah kissed me and I locked my arms around his neck as his tightened around my waist.

"Was this. The. Surprise?" I asked between a kiss when I had a chance.

"It's not surprise I love you, thought I'd show it," he said stopping for a moment.

"Noah... I've never done this..." I said.

"Okay, we don't have to," he said and ran his fingers through my hair. I wanted to... so bad. We were alone, together... happy and every part of me wanted to show him how much I loved him. "But I want to... with you... I trust you."

"Are you sure?"

"Absolutely."

March

"Noah!" I called.

"He's not back yet!" I heard Robert call from the living room. He was relaxing before he had to leave for work. I decided to make my way to Noah's room and get comfortable. Meaning waiting in his bed. We hadn't had sex since Valentine's Day and I was ready to go again. As I sat my bag down by his desk, I removed my shirt and dropped it, knocking down a stack of papers. I picked them up and noticed an envelope from UCLA. I opened it and read that he was accepted. Was he ever going to tell me? This was mailed back in January!

"Babe, dad said you were-."

I turned, and Noah was smirking.

"Oh, okay… um, what do you have in mind?" Noah asked and sauntered over to me.

"UCLA?" I asked. Noah looked at the letter and took it from me.

"You were going through my things?" he asked.

"No, I knocked some papers over when I came in. Did you plan on telling me? Or did you just want to use me? Tell me you love me, fuck me, and leave. Hm? Is that it?" I yelled.

"Why? WHY would you think that?" he yelled back.

"You didn't think maybe we should talk about this? You can't just tell someone you love them, then leave! That's not how love works!"

"Okay, please. Love guru, tell me how it works because I'm

sure all seven billion people in the world would LOVE to FUCK-ING know!"

Silence.

Dead silence.

Noah took a deep breath and I put my shirt back on.

"Aria..."

"Don't!"

"I shouldn't have yelled like that."

"Stop, I'm done."

"No, you're not. Let's sit down and talk, okay?" he asked. I grabbed my bag and Noah followed me out. "You don't have a car-,"

"I'll walk."

"It's like ten miles, and it's freezing. I'm not letting you walk-."

"Too bad."

"Aria-."

"I said we're done, Noah. Keep it up and I'll call the cops," I said. The tears were filling my eyes, but I refused to let him see me cry. Noah backed off and I continued down the road.

I wasn't stupid. I heard him start the Jeep and follow me home. He still texted me and asked if I got home safe. Then sent an I love you and finished with a goodnight. I overreacted. It's a rude awakening how fast our lives pass us by. It may only be March, but graduation was two months away, then summer vacation and BAM, he's gone. I don't know if I could make that work.

April

A funny thing about love is... we never really know for sure. But I knew. Noah didn't give up. Texting me, sending me actual handwritten letters in the mail about his day- by sending I mean before school he'd stop at the house and slip them in the mailbox. I caught him one morning. I found someone to keep. But I left him.

"Aria, there's been an emergency," my mom snapped me from my thoughts.

"What's wrong?" I asked and quickly slid on my shoes.

"It's your grandmother, come on!" she said and began frantically rushing to her room to find her shoes and a coat. I followed her out to the car as tears were flying from her face and she drove us to the hospital. She was speeding, but luckily, we didn't get pulled over as she parked and practically ran inside. My dad was at work, but my mom said he would be on his way as she walked straight into the room, leaving me in the hallway. I stood in the hall, crying in fear. This could be bad. Noah texted me a typical good morning and I called him.

"Morning," he said.

"Noah, I need you," I cried.

"Woah, what's wrong? Where are you?"

"I'm at the hospital. Grandma is here... I don't know what's going on... Can you come?" I asked.

"Yeah, text me what floor and room," he said, and we hung up. I sent him the information and waited for either him or my mother, but fifteen minutes later he came running down the hall toward me.

"Have you heard anything?" he asked.

"No," I said. He pulled me into his arms and kissed the top of my head. "Noah, I'm sorry."

"About what?"

"The way I acted. You didn't deserve-."

"Shh, apology accepted. Relax," he said and rubbed my back. "I love you," he said.

"I love you, Noah," I cried. He squeezed his arms around me when my mom came out, crying. On April 8th, 2019 my grandmother passed away.

Graduation

Noah and I showed up at graduation early so he could meet with everyone beforehand and get lined up. I sat down and saved seats for my family and Noah's.

His dad came in first and smiled when he saw me.

"Morning, Aria," he said and kissed my cheek.

"Morning," I smiled and watched as his grandparents came in, not long followed by my parents.

We took our seats as they began walking in. When Noah came in, he sat down and smiled at us. His dad was taking photos, as was my mom. Now it was his turn.

"Noah Turner. Noah's been the school quarterback for two years and plans to... major in Photojournalism at UCLA in the fall." They announced.

"What?" his dad asked. I froze too. Last I knew he was still deciding.

"I'm as shocked as you are," I said. Noah took his diploma and posed for a photo with the principal and superintendent before walking off the stage and avoiding eye contact with me and his dad. I wasn't mad. I'm happy for him. And now this summer was going to be the best one ever.

June

Noah and his dad had a rough week after graduation. Noah decided to fit football into his plans while focusing on his major. His dad wasn't happy but still agreed to pay his tuition. Then came the difficult part for us. But Noah didn't want to talk about it. The last few months had to be perfect.

We sat in Rex's Diner and I looked down at the menu the waitress sat in front of me.

"What can I start you two off with to drink?" she asked.

"I'll take a water, she'll take coffee. Can we get some cream?" he asked. She nodded as he looked over the menu and she walked away. I kept looking up at him. He brushed his hair to the side today and wore a nice black polo shirt. He looked super cute. The waitress sat down his water, my mug, and a bowl of creamer.

"Do you still need a few minutes?" she asked.

"Yes, please," I said as Noah began putting one creamer in my mug. I watched as he added three sugars and stirred it before sliding it across the table. "You remembered?"

"Yeah. And I kinda wanted to show off," he admitted.

"That you know how I like my coffee?" I laughed. He nodded, and we ended up ordering the same thing we usually got. Noah looked out the window at the parking lot and turned back to me with a light smile.

"You thought about applying for college yet?" Noah sked. That was the last concern on my mind.

"Um, no."

"Why not?"

"I'm more worried about us right now-."

"No. Focus on school. Okay? We're fine. When I leave-."

"Noah, you said we weren't going to talk about it until August."

"I know," he said and tapped his fingers against the table.

"What do you want for your birthday? It's in a few days," I smiled.

"Really?"

"What? You have to want something?"

"I have you, I don't need anything else."

"Something for your dorm?"

"Okay, probably, but you're not responsible for that," he smiled.

"Fine, I'll figure it out on my own," I shrugged. Noah sighed and reached across the table and held my hands.

"Let's enjoy the summer, okay?"

"Okay," I smiled and felt my phone buzz. I pulled one of my hands away and took my phone out of my pocket to see a text from Christina.

"Party @ Ryker's tonight. Let's go."

"Who is it?" Noah asked.

"Christina. Ryker's throwing a party tonight-."

"Let's go."

"What?"

"We're official now. Let me take you to a party before I leave."

"Are you sure?"

"Yes. It'll be fun," he winked as our food showed up and he

pulled his other hand away.

We pulled up outside Ryker's house later that night and people were standing in the front yard talking as Noah parked along the road.

"Wow, he sure knows how to get the word out," Noah commented as we walked across the yard and up to the front door.

"Noah!"

A few guys caught Noah instantly, so I continued inside to search for Christina. I stopped when Madison and I made eye contact from across the house. I had heard she wasn't very happy about Noah and me… and I was actually a little scared of her.

"Hey!"

I let out a sigh of relief when I heard Christina's voice and turned to my left to see her approach.

"Hey!" I smiled and hugged her.

"Jackie said she'll be over in a bit. She brought her new boyfriend."

"Good! I'm glad she's happy," I responded.

"Yeah… but you know who isn't."

"Yeah, she saw me already."

"Think she'll do anything?"

"Maybe. Noah and I discussed it already."

"You talk about him like you've been married for years," Christina teased with a gag.

"Shut up. We talk… communicate. That's how you keep a relationship," I rolled my eyes as we walked over to the kitchen counter and grabbed a drink. I looked up to see Noah looking around the room before his eyes landed on me. He made his way over and grabbed a bottle of water.

"Guys!"

Ryker came over and I smiled.

"Hey! Crazy party," Christina said as Noah put his arm around me and joined us.

"Yeah, I'm impressed," Noah added.

"Thank you. Both schools were excited to show up," Ryker shrugged and drank from his cup.

"I met with your team out front," Noah nodded.

"Yeah, that reminds me. Aria, Madison wanted to speak with you," Ryker said.

"Oh, I'm good." I said and sipped from my cup.

"You sure?"

"Yep."

Christina took Ryker's hand and sat her cup down.

"Let's dance!"

They disappeared in the crowd of people and I turned to Noah.

"You okay?" he asked and tucked a strand of hair behind my ear.

"Mhm," I nodded and finished my cup.

"Could we just go back to your house? I thought this would be fun..."

"We can dance? Or is it Madison?"

"I'm uncomfortable. I feel like she's just over my shoulder," I frowned.

"Okay. Let's go back to my place," he said lightly and took my hand.

"Noah!"

I looked and saw Cadin. Noah turned to me and I sighed.

"Go ahead."

He smiled and walked over to his friends as I made my way out of the house.

"Aria, wait up!"

Oh no.

I turned, and Madison looked at me.

"Hey, I wanted to talk to you," she sighed.

"What?"

"Well, I was talking with Cadin the other day and Noah's such an ass! I can't believe you're okay with what he said about overweight women. Even about you!"

She was lying.

"What do you mean?" I asked anyhow.

"The guys have made it a goal to date heavier girls, so they can have sex as much as they want. Since apparently heavier girls are harder to get pregnant? I don't know, they were looking at articles the last week of classes."

I looked over at Cadin and Noah to see Cadin's new girl-friend was heavier than me. I remembered back to the night Cadin and I went out. This had to be true.

"Right. Well, thanks Madison," I spat and continued out of the house, waiting by Noah's motorcycle.

About ten minutes passed before Noah came out of the house and approached me.

"Ready?" he smiled.

"Yeah, just take me home."

"What? I thought you'd want to stay over?"

"No, I wanna go home."

"Is everything okay?"

"I don't know. Let's just go." I shrugged as we climbed on the bike.

Noah pulled into the driveway and I hopped off the bike trying to process what Madison had said.

"We can talk about whatever is going on. Only way this will work is if you talk to me," Noah stated. I stared at him, watching as his eyebrows furrowed in concern and his pink lips were pressed tight in a straight line.

"I think I'm just tired," I lied.

"That's a complete lie, but okay," he sighed and rolled his eyes.

"I'll call you tomorrow," I hesitated.

"Okay. Goodnight," he sighed.

"Night." I said and turned to walk inside.

When I woke up the next morning, I thought I'd have calmed down. I texted Noah I was coming over and texted Christina to pick me up, so I could run everything past her first.

"Madison said that?" Christina asked as I sat in the passenger seat.

"Yep."

"You don't seriously believe her?"

I shrugged, and Christina eyed me.

"Aria, you've been with Noah since September. He didn't push you into anything. Why would you believe that?"

"When I went out with Cadin he made a comment-."

"That was Cadin. Not Noah. Just because they are friends doesn't mean Noah has the same idiotic mindset. Look, if that was Noah's intention, he'd dump you before he leaves and not try to make this work."

"He still has time…"

"Stop! God, if you keep acting like this, he will dump you! Noah cares about you! Just go over, say you were having a rough night and enjoy the time you have left with your boyfriend!"

"Okay."

Christina dropped me off and Noah was already outside waiting for me.

"Morning," he grinned and pulled me in for a kiss.

"Morning," I responded. He waved to Christina and we walked inside.

"I have a few movies out if you just want to relax?" Noah asked as I stood in the entryway. "Or not?" he laughed in confusion. Usually I'd make myself at home and today I just stood. "Something was wrong last night…"

"I know I'm fat-."

"Woah, where'd this come from?" Noah stopped me right away.

"There's a few stupid articles online that say if you're overweight it can be more difficult to conceive-."

"What?" Noah's eyes widened as I spoke. I realized he clearly didn't have a clue about what I was saying, and I ran my hand over my face.

"I'm so stupid. Never mind."

"Um. no. Now I want an explanation," Noah said. I stood there, and Noah waited, a stern look across his features.

"Last night, Madison came up to me-."

"Jesus Christ!" Noah exclaimed and rolled his eyes. "We talked about this, Aria!"

"I know, but she just knew how to get under my skin. Noah, I moved schools three times because of how I looked!"

"What do you mean?" he faltered.

"Noah, I was bullied constantly about my weight! The first school I didn't participate in gym because when I ran boys always made comments about my boobs-."

"That's not a bad thing..."

"Noah," I glared.

"Sorry."

"Then there were comments about my stomach jiggling. School two, my thighs jiggled and I got a boyfriend who told everyone about my stretchmarks on my stomach and thighs... said they were like purple wrinkles and people thought it was disgusting and hilarious. School three, the quarterback thought it'd be funny to "date" me and secretly take photos of me eating. The football team made a page called "Lil Piglet Aria" and it was photos of me eating or in my PE shorts."

"Aria, I had no clue-."

"I never wanted to tell you this, Noah! I never wanted anyone to know. But Madison's comment brought back so many memories..." I trailed off and didn't realize I was crying until Noah wrapped his arms around me.

"Shh," Noah hushed and held me tight as the tears fell at an alarming rate.

"You are one of the most beautiful girls I have ever met. Don't doubt us because of other assholes who've been in your life. I love every part of you. And this..." he gripped onto my hips and looked down at my body. "This is who you are. I wouldn't change a thing about you. Your heart is pure gold. Why would I care about your stomach?" Noah asked and wiped the tears from my face.

"I'm nothing like Jackie," I whispered.

"Jackie doesn't mean shit to me anymore, Aria. Only you," he said and held his hand against my cheek, carefully wiping away tears pooling under my eyes with his thumb. I took his other hand in mine and squeezed it tight. "I love you."

"I love you too," I whimpered, and he squeezed me to his chest, kissing the top of my head.

"Let's go watch a movie, okay?"

"Yeah. Okay," I said, and he led me into the living room.

June 19th

"Thanks for dropping me off, Mom," I said as we sat in the driveway of Noah's house.

"Yeah, no problem. I do need to talk to you about something," she said. I looked at her and she seemed slightly uncomfortable.

"I know you both like each other and just make sure if you decide to…" she trailed off and I cringed.

"Ew, yeah. Okay, mom, I get it," I jumped and opened the door.

"Just be safe!" she called. I shut the door and waved as I held Noah's gift in my hands. I knew how much he loved taking photos and I found a lens that can attach to his phone's camera. I walked inside and Robert stood in the kitchen.

"Morning," he said.

"Is Noah up yet?" I asked.

"Nope. Would you like to do the honors?" Robert asked.

"Sure."

I sat his gift on the counter and walked upstairs to his room. I knocked lightly before opening the door to see him sleeping peacefully. I walked around the bed and climbed in beside him. He stirred and opened his eyes slowly.

"Morning," he mumbled and pulled me into his chest, closing his eyes again.

"Happy Birthday," I said.

"Mhm… ugh, right," he groaned and stretched lightly.

"Wanna come downstairs? Looks like your dad is making brunch."

"Ugh, yeah… sure."

I got up as Noah swung his legs out of the bed and pointed to his dresser.

"Could you grab a shirt and pants?" he asked lazily. I laughed and walked over opening a drawer of all his shirts. I grabbed a grey shirt and when it unfolded, I saw a sugar skull on the right sleeve. I shut the drawer and opened the next one, jeans. I grabbed a random pair and tossed them at him. "Thank you."

We both reached the kitchen and Robert had three plates out and began plating pancakes. Noah made his way to the fridge and poured all of us some orange juice. I sat at the counter and Noah joined me handing me a glass.

"Happy Birthday, Noah," Robert smiled. Noah nodded and noticed my gift on the counter that sat now with two others.

"I told you guys not to get anything," Noah smiled lightly as we ate.

"What's a birthday without at least one gift?" his dad asked as he joined us and started eating. I passed my gift to Noah as he ate, and he peeked at me. He smiled and sat down his fork, opening my gift.

"Oh, cool. I didn't know they made these," he said and started reading the box. His dad looked too and seemed impressed.

"That's interesting," he said. Noah smiled at me and leaned over to give me a quick kiss.

"Thank you."

"Hand him the bigger one next," Robert said. I did so and read the tag, From: Dad.

Noah opened it to see UCLA sweats and a t-shirt.

"Thanks, Dad," Noah smiled, and his dad gripped his shoulder. I looked at the tag on the next one and my breath hitched.

To: Noah

Love, Mom

"This next one... I was told to wait till right before college, but I think this is a good time," Robert said. Noah looked confused as Robert nodded to me. I handed Noah the box and as soon as he read the tag, he stared at it for a moment. He opened the wrapping paper and looked at the wooden box for another moment. He took a deep breath and quickly wiped a tear from his eyes as he opened the box. He pulled out a pair of earrings, a photo of the family: Noah, Robert, and his mom at a park when Noah was younger, a letter, and a thick gold ring.

"Your mom wore that around her neck. She found it at some antique shop and put it on a chain. She figured that might be something you'd like," Robert said. Noah slid it on his middle finger before putting everything else back but the letter.

"We'll give you a minute," I said and nodded to Robert. We went into the living room and sat down for about fifteen minutes.

"Aria?" Noah called. I looked at Robert and he nodded or me to go. I walked in and Noah handed me the letter, pulling me into his arms. I wrapped my arms around him as he sobbed quietly into my chest.

"September 29th, 2015

Noah Francis,

I wanted to make sure you know how proud I am of you. Your dad may seem like your biggest enemy at times, but he loves you with everything he has. He's taking over my role and making sure you're healthy and safe. He's going through everything you are. Be there for each other and take care of each other, for me.

I know you had talked to me about college and how you wanted to travel the world and take many photos. I hope that is something you will do.

I promise to be there every step of the way. Even when you feel alone, I assure you I am right there. You've been visiting me every day and as much as I love seeing you, I hope you make a lot of new friends.

You talk about Jackie a lot... I hope that turns into a dream come true. If not, know that there will be a girl (or boy, I don't care either way) who will make you feel like the center of the universe. They will love you in your worst moments and always be there no matter how difficult the situation. You're not going to have a problem finding that person, Noah. You have a big heart and I love that about you. You were my greatest gift.

You're making me very proud.

Always & Forever.

I love you,

Mom"

I sat the letter down and hugged him tight as he started to calm down. He pulled away, wiped his eyes, and cleared his throat.

"Sorry," he said.

"It's fine. Are you alright?" I asked. He nodded and looked behind me. I turned, and Robert came back in.

"I thought we could watch some TV today? I have to pick up a cake in about an hour..."

"Let's visit mom," Noah said. Robert nodded and grabbed his wallet and keys. "And pick up some flowers on the way," he added. Robert didn't protest as we all grabbed our phones and walked out to the garage. Robert climbed in the driver's seat and I was surprised when Noah hopped in the back with me. He held my hand on the drive to the store. The three of us picked out some flowers and we were back on the road again. Robert pulled off the trail and we all climbed out as Noah led us to the tombstone.

Carly Turner

April 4th, 1969- October 5th, 2015

Noah sat the flowers down and returned to my side, locking our fingers together. I looked up at the side of his face and noticed he had a small smile on his face before turning to look down at me.

"Thank you," he mumbled to me.

"For what?"

"Being here," he said and hugged me again.

July

I sat on the couch in the living room as my dad was channel surfing. We heard Noah's motorcycle pull into the driveway and I stood up to answer the door.

"Hey!" I smiled as he ran up to the door with two tickets. "What're those?"

"Two tickets to see Fall Out Boy tomorrow night! Cadin can't go so he gave them to me. What do you say?"

"Where's the concert?" I asked.

"Allstate Arena in Chicago."

"That's a two-hour drive or longer..."

"We can stay in town. There's a hotel across the way. Dad's okay with it. Mr. Boyd?" Noah asked turning to look at my dad. I turned as well, and he looked from me to Noah.

"Okay," he said.

"What? Really?" I asked with a huge smile.

"Yeah."

"Oh my god!" I jumped and hugged Noah in excitement.

"I'll pick you up in the morning and we can drop our things off at the hotel," he said.

"Okay, sounds great!"

"Alright," Noah smiled and pecked my lips before rushing out the front door.

I had my bag packed right away and sat it in the living room.

Noah's Jeep pulled in and I said goodbye to my parents before running out and climbing in the Jeep.

"Got everything?" Noah asked.

"Yeah, double checked twice."

"That means you checked four times…"

"Exactly," I confirmed. Noah laughed and pulled out of the driveway. He put on Fall Out Boy's older music as we drove.

"This is going to be a lot of fun." Noah said as we pulled onto the highway.

"I've actually never left town like this with anyone besides my parents," I revealed.

"I'm glad I get to take you. There's a Chipotle and Culver's by the arena if you want to grab food beforehand?" he asked.

"Yeah. Chipotle would probably be easier, we can grab it when we get in town, so we don't have to leave several times?" I suggested as the traffic already began to slow. Noah was a fast driver overall, so I was sure he'd figure out a way to keep us moving.

"Aria, wake up."

"Hm?" I opened my eyes and Noah was laughing at me. I looked down and a Chipotle bag sat on my lap. I didn't realize we were already at the hotel.

"I already checked in. Are you ready?"

"Yeah. I can't believe I fell asleep," I laughed lightly.

"That's alright. More energy for the show," Noah grinned as he grabbed our bags and I carried the food.

We got into our room and climbed on the bed before we started eating. I didn't even have to tell Noah my order which made me grin as we ate. His smile was big, and he looked like a child.

"You're in a really good mood," I commented.

"Yeah! We're out of town. My dad's not here. We're going to a concert. I'm with the love of my life..." Noah shook his head as he took another bite of his burrito.

"You can keep going..." I teased as he listed reasons for his excitement.

"This is my first concert too..."

"Well if you finish eating, we can get ready and go stand outside."

We didn't get back to our room until a little after midnight because of how many people were filing out. We even had to make sure to use the crosswalks, so people didn't hit us. Our voices were scratchy from screaming and Noah keep this arm around me as we walked back to the hotel.

"That was so much fun!" he gushed as we entered the lobby of the hotel.

"I was so happy they played more of their older things!"

Noah unlocked the door and I collapsed onto the bed right away.

"Get changed!" Noah laughed and rolled his eyes at me. "How can you be tired? You slept the whole way here!"

"Fine," I groaned and began removing my clothes. I changed into a St. Andrew's football shirt and shorts as Noah slid on his plaid sleep pants. "If you didn't sweat so much, I could wear your shirt and we'd be like the cute couples in movies."

"Nice try," he commented and pulled back the blankets. I fell in bed and he dove in beside me pulling me into his arms. I laughed, and he pecked my lips. As soon as his arms wrapped around me and my head hit the pillow I was out like a light.

August

Not many relationships go this well in high school. And not many high school relationships last. As August began, I tried to limit my time with Noah before he left. However, he made it difficult. He wanted me to come over for dinner, or to watch a movie, or my favorite- he couldn't sleep. He'd come and pick me up in the middle of the night, just to have me beside him. The fair was this weekend, so we decided to go, and we'd leave for the airport in the morning.

I walked downstairs and stopped when I heard my parents talking in hushed tones.

"Is she going to handle this? I mean, he's leaving. It's about the same as a break-up, isn't it?" my mom asked.

"Who knows. We've never had this happen. She should be fine," my dad answered. I hit my foot against the floor as I walked into the room and my parents smiled.

"Hey, honey," my mom said.

"Hi," I responded.

"Noah's picking you up soon, right?" she asked.

"Yep," I answered with a small smile. Was I upset Noah was leaving? Sure. But I've known he was leaving for months. The familiar sound of Noah's motorcycle pulled me out of my trance. "See you tonight," I said to my parents. I walked out the front door and saw Noah on his bike, holding out a helmet to me.

We arrived at the fairgrounds and got our wristbands to go in. Christina had texted me saying she wanted to say goodbye to

Noah before he left, and I was sure other people would be stopping us to say goodbye to him as well. Noah saw a few of his friends and started talking to them as I watched a young boy play a game. It was the one with the baseball and knocking over the bottles. He wasn't throwing far enough, and he motioned to the stuffed animal wall but the vendor in charge shook his head.

"Noah!" I said and hit his arm.

"What?" he asked, and I motioned over to the boy. Noah and I walked over, and the vendor's eyes landed on Noah.

"You want a stuffed animal?" I asked the boy.

"Gator!" he pointed. I looked at Noah and he handed the man a ticket. The boy watched Noah fascinated by how tall he was. Noah played sports his whole life, so I wanted him to do this. If I did, he wouldn't have gotten anything. Noah won and pointed at the alligator. The vendor handed it to him, and Noah squatted down to the boys level and handed it to him.

"There ya go, man. High-five for effort!" Noah said and the boy hit his hand before running off to find his guardian.

"Thank you," I said.

"He wanted a gator!" Noah said back. I laughed as we walked down the trail.

"Noah!"

We turned and Cadin was at the basketball booths. Noah walked over, and I stepped away as they challenged each other. I looked around for Christina when a hand landed on my shoulder and I jumped.

"You look a lot like this girl I know..." Christina teased.

"Hey!" I laughed and hugged her.

"Where's Noah?" she asked, and I pointed across the way. "Oh. This is gonna be hard for you, isn't it?"

"I hope not. I heard my parents this morning saying it might be like a break-up," I frowned.

"It might seem that way. Noah will make sure to talk to you, though. I don't think you have anything to worry about," she shrugged as a few bells went off and Noah beat Cadin. They laughed and hugged as Noah returned and noticed Christina.

"Chrissy!" he grinned and opened his arms to her.

"Hey Noah," she smiled and hugged him. "Don't hurt her or I will fly out there myself and hunt you down."

"I know you would," Noah smiled.

"There's a magician in Barn 4 at two. You guys wanna go?" she asked.

"I don't really believe in magic," Noah revealed.

"What? Noah, c'mon! We have to go!" I pouted.

"I mean, we can go but it's all bullshit," he said.

"This will be good," Christina laughed. We stopped and got some lemonade before walking to the barn and taking our seats. A man came out on the small stage and waved to everyone.

"Hello! Welcome to the show. My name is Alec Bridges and I need to know before we really get started… Who here doesn't believe in magic?" he asked.

"Ah, this guy! Right here!" Christina said and pointed at Noah.

"Okay. Sir, please come on up," he said. Noah glared at Christina as he walked up, and Alec pulled out a deck of cards.

"What's your name?" Alec asked him.

"Noah,"

"Alright. Noah, can you confirm all these cards are different?" Alec asked spreading a deck out before him. He nodded and Alec went on, "Okay. I would like you to pick one card."

Noah picked a card and looked at it.

"Go tell someone in the audience your card," Alec said. Noah ran up to me and said,

"This is bullshit. Nine of hearts."

I laughed, and he returned in front of Alec and placed the card in the deck. Alec sat the deck down and put his hand up to Noah.

"Are you right or left handed?" he asked.

"Right," Noah answered. They clasped onto each other's hand and Alec faced the crowd.

"Alright, now take in a few deep breaths. One... two... three, exhale. Okay. I'm going to guess and say your card is a red card, am I right?" Alec asked.

"Yes." Noah answered.

"Okay, another guess. Your card is a higher card... above seven?"

"Yeah..." Noah said.

"Okay, another guess... your card is not a picture card as in a jack, queen, or king?"

"No," Noah confirmed.

"Okay... I'm gonna say your card is a diamond..."

"No," Noah said. The man let go of Noah's hand and faced the crowd again.

"Alright everyone, in my back pocket I have an envelope and I wrote something inside. Noah, please open and read the note," Alec said. Noah took the small envelope and opened it. He eyed Alec before reading,

"Noah you are thinking of the nine of hearts," Noah's mouth fell open as he looked at Alec in shock.

"Was that your card?"

"Yeah," Noah answered, and everyone clapped. Alec

thanked Noah and they shook hands as Noah made his way back over to us and sat down.

"It's just bullshit?" I asked him.

"Yep." He said, and I laughed.

The show ended, and Christina went off on her own. Noah and I decided to grab some food from one of the trucks and we sat at a picnic table.

"Was this a fun date?" Noah asked as he broke a piece off my funnel cake.

"Yes, a lot of fun," I smiled.

"Dad said we'll pick you up around eight tomorrow morning. Gives me enough time to go through security."

"Right," I nodded. I took a bite of my food and he grabbed my hand.

"You've got some powdered sugar..." he grinned and wiped it off my face. I laughed, and he took another piece.

Noah made sure we rode the ferris wheel before we left and the whole time I gripped onto his hand. Was I afraid of heights? Yes. Did I tell him? Nope.

Noah dropped me off and he walked me up to the door.

"I'll see you in the morning," I trailed off.

"Yeah. I'll text you before we leave," he said.

"Okay. Goodnight, Noah."

"Goodnight, Aria," he said and kissed me. I pulled away and smiled before walking inside. As soon as the door shut, the tears fell.

I'd be lying if I said I didn't cry myself to sleep that night. In my mind, it felt stupid. He'd be back on holidays. We can Face-Time... but it still felt like he would be missing. I made sure to get up, shower, and look nice. His last impression of me would be the one he remembers. As I was eating a bowl of Fruity Pebbles, he texted me saying they were on their way. I finished eating and just in time as the car horn sounded in the driveway. My parents were still in bed, so I let myself out where Noah stood outside the car with a jacket in his hands. His leather jacket. I smiled as I walked up to him.

"What's with the jacket?" I asked.

"It's your jacket now," he said and put it around me on my shoulders. I clutched onto it as he opened the backseat door and we both climbed in.

The whole drive was silent. The radio was very low on the pop channel and my head was against Noah's chest the whole way. He occasionally leaned down and pressed a kiss to the top of my head. He hadn't touched his phone, and I didn't either. I was scared if I moved, we'd be at the airport quicker. When we did arrive, I climbed out and helped Robert with Noah's bags. We were able to walk with him for most of the way, then came the part I dreaded.

"Bye, Dad," Noah said and hugged Robert. He smiled and when he looked down at me, I felt my tears in my eyes. "No, please don't cry..." Noah sighed when he saw me wipe away a tear that had escaped.

"Sorry," I sighed and with a blink of my eye, the tears flew. I sniffled, and Noah pulled me into his arms, tight. Tighter than ever. Wait, maybe I was the one squeezing? I loosened my grip as he let go and held my face in his hands.

"I'm only a phone call away," he said. I nodded, and he kissed the top of my head. "I love you."

"I love you too," I responded.

"Bye," he said and adjusted the bag he held on his shoulder. He turned around and I felt Robert put his hand on my shoulder.

"Are you ready?"

"I just wanna watch him go," I said. Noah walked on and when he disappeared from view, I turned to Robert. "Okay."

Made in the USA
Lexington, KY
25 April 2019